twisted endings

A collection of short stories with unexpected endings

samyra alexander

contents

before you read...

Trigger warnings include murder, rape, mental illness, suicide, and physical assault.

family meeting

. . .

WHILE MY HUSBAND, Richard, drives through Skid Row, I stare out the window in awe. Culture shock is what I'm experiencing. This couldn't be America. On each block, homeless people are everywhere: lounging in chairs and posting against buildings. From what I can tell, they don't have jobs or any significant business, seeing as it's noon. What has the state of California done with the taxpayers' dollars? Back home in Indianapolis, we have homeless people, but not to this extent. This isn't our first trip to Los Angeles, but we have never been to Skid Row. I don't fully understand why we're here today. We visited the city last year when we dropped our only child, Gerolyn, off at U.S.C. for her first year of college. She's the best child anyone could ask for.

Richard and I had tried for years to get pregnant, only for me to have four miscarriages. When she came into our lives, we vowed to give her the world. She'd been an honor roll student since she began school, so we weren't shocked when she graduated at seventeen with a full scholarship to U.S.C. Gerolyn struggles with social anxiety. I hope college life will enhance her confidence. She fears strangers and only speaks if they speak first; her friends initiated relationships with her. She had a boyfriend in high school if you could call him that. Richard hooked her up with a guy from the church and took them to the

"

movies and to eat. Gerolyn held hands with the boy but always appeared uncomfortable. I doubt they kissed. She's a late bloomer, which concerns me since she'll miss opportunities because she's shy. Since she didn't go through a rebellious phase and loves me and Richard, I shouldn't complain.

When she went off to college, she called us often, but one month ago, the calls stopped. We didn't hear from her unless we called. She refused to video chat but swore she was doing well and busy with classes. We didn't believe her, but without proof, we stopped hounding her. We were surprised when she called two days ago, sounding unlike her normal happy self. She said we had to come to Los Angeles. She was in trouble, and the police could soon be involved—it was a matter of life and death. When we demanded more details, she said she might've said too much already and that she'd fill us in once we got to Los Angeles. After she hung up on us, we called back, but she wouldn't answer. Her only communication was texts saying she'd explain everything soon.

Richard wanted to call her college to request a wellness check, but I didn't want administration involved without us first knowing what was going on. The school might jump to conclusions and threaten to kick her out; I'd be devastated if her life were ruined, and I could've prevented it. My hesitancy to contact the school caused a huge argument between Richard and me that resulted in me sleeping in the guest room. Before bed that night, I prayed to Mother Mary for Gerolyn, who has never been in trouble. The next day, once Richard was no longer upset, he called his friends at the holiness church where he belongs and asked them to pray. Luckily, we had money saved since last-minute flights are expensive. As if I weren't stressed enough about my child, Richard complained until we boarded the plane about how much overtime he'd have to work to make up for the cost of the tickets.

I'm uncertain why we're meeting Gerolyn downtown because her school isn't in this part of the city, but she insisted we meet her here and refused to give more details. This new secretive nature of hers is detestable. I'm not one for surprises.

Richard parks the car in front of a homeless shelter. "This can't be the right address," he says, staring at the loads of people hanging out.

Grabbing my St. Michael necklace for comfort, I say, "This is the address." I'm scared to get out of the car. I've never seen this many homeless people. Not far from the car, a man is talking to himself and punching at the air. I pray aloud, "Angel Michael, protect my family and give us strength." I stop when Richard interrupts me with his negativity.

"Kelly, don't start talking to angels. They take commandments from God, not man. You're wasting your time. If you want to pray about something, ask God to send me back the money I paid for our flights with. If Gerolyn got us out here for some foolishness, she's getting a summer job to reimburse us." For him to think Gerolyn would bring us to California with little notice and it is not an emergency is ridiculous. He makes good money but is stingy.

I love my husband, but our biggest sources of contention are religion and money. If finances and God aren't involved, he's kind and relaxed. We both found God after years of marriage, yet we serve Him at different churches. I assumed time would cause Richard to accept I'm Catholic and would never convert to his faith; I'm impatiently waiting for the day he does. He considers my religion pagan. I pray to Mother Mary and the angels and believe deceased saints watch over me and my family, while Richard is convinced his religion is the only way to God.

Instead of arguing with him, I get out of the car to find my child, and so does Richard. We text her, and seconds later, she comes around the corner, and we hug and kiss her. I don't like that Gerolyn is trembling in my arms. Whatever the reason we're here isn't good. She shakes whenever she must tell us something she fears we won't like. Now isn't the time to criticize her appearance, but she's disheveled. If I didn't know any better, I'd think she was homeless. Is she? Why else would we be on Skid Row and racking our brains about what is so urgent we had to fly here immediately? My child looks unloved. Her hair is in a messy ponytail, and her T-shirt and shorts are too big, even though she's gained weight. Now that I think about it, she couldn't be homeless as round as she is. She hasn't missed a meal. The weight must be a result of the freshman fifteen, the fifteen pounds most college students gain their first year.

"I don't want to talk here in front of everyone." She waves to us to follow her. "We need privacy for a family meeting. It means a lot to me that you both came."

"We didn't have much of a choice. What trouble have you gotten into?" Richard says what I am thinking.

"I'll explain everything in a minute." Her shaky words provide no comfort.

Something about this doesn't feel right. Why isn't she on campus? I turn to Richard, hoping he can help me make sense of things. He grabs my hand as if to say he is as clueless as me and he needs my strength.

After turning the corner, I clutch my purse tight. There are more homeless people on this street, and some are on drugs. I imagine one of them will knock us over the head and rob us. It's obvious we aren't from here. Ahead of us is a woman sitting in a lawn chair outside a tent, cooling herself with a handheld, battery-operated fan. She has a table on the side of the tent with things for sale. This is the last place I expect to find a pop-up business. If I were homeless, I doubt I'd be motivated to make money. Although I'm not a drinker, I imagine I'd be in my tent, drinking the pain away. Bottled water, chips, hats, and socks are on the sales table. No fans. It's so hot, I want to ask if she has another fan inside her tent I could buy. Instead, I stare at the woman, wondering how she ended up here. Rather than scowl at me for staring at her like something foreign, she smiles as if she's accustomed to strangers gawking at her and saying nothing. Forcing a smile in return, I accept the free bottled water she hands me, and I thank her. When I try to give her money, she refuses. Behind her eyes is wisdom. She doesn't know me, but I feel she's picking up on the fact that I'm distressed. My bet is she's a mother too.

Seconds later, Gerolyn stops in front of a tent that looks made of tarp and other materials. It's a makeshift house.

"What are we doing here?" I ask. It's time she gave us answers. She couldn't call and say it was a life-and-death matter and keep us in suspense.

"Start talking now." Normally, I would tell Richard to chill with the bass in his voice, but I understand his frustration.

Disregarding us, Gerolyn pulls the tarp back, enters, and holds it open for Richard and me. She can't be serious about us going in there. Why is she even going in? Is this a school project she wants feedback on? This is ridiculous.

Not knowing what to expect, I enter, and there are folding chairs, a small table, and buckets. From the outside, the place looked smaller.

"Sit," Gerolyn says. After everyone is seated, Gerolyn avoids eye contact as if she's afraid to talk. I grab my necklace for strength. Is she homeless? Or on drugs? Both? Did the school kick her out of the dorm?

"I brought you all here because I'm no longer in school. They took back the scholarship when they found I was selling drugs on campus."

I'm now living my worst nightmare. What have I done to deserve this?

Richard says, "What the hell do you mean? Your mama and I didn't sacrifice all we did for you to leave Indiana to come to college and sell drugs. Your scholarship doesn't pay for your clothes and daily needs; your mother and I do. If the school expels you, everything we've done for you would've been for nothing." Richard is already a loud talker, but he's screaming, and if he doesn't calm down, I fear he'll lose his voice. "Are you stupid? Weren't there enough drugs in Indiana for you to slang if this is the life you wanted to live? You had a free ride to school and worked on campus. Why would you sell drugs?"

This is too much to take in, and I'm at a loss for words. My good girl, who never gave us a day's problem, the valedictorian of her class, is a drug dealer. This couldn't be true. She was socially awkward her whole life; selling drugs requires social skills she doesn't have. Someone must be trafficking her. I can't bring myself to respond to her, not now. I want to curse and throw something to express to Gerolyn how much she's let me and her father down.

"I know it's not what you expect from me. I'm sorry. I met a guy who loves me, and it's his family business, so it was only right I helped. You two always said relationships require teamwork."

I was right. Someone is pimping her out and making her sell drugs. She's so clueless about life, she assumes he loves her.

"And you thought that meant follow a man down an illegal path? We raised you better than that." Richard nudges me, looking annoyed at my silence. "Kelly, say something. Are you hearing this?"

Does he assume I'm deaf? Of course, I hear her. I'm trying to understand what happened to my child and how I can fix her. It's wrong to leave Richard alone to deal with our child. "You're coming home. This is all my fault. I should've never let the elementary school skip you a grade. At seventeen, you are too young and naïve to be in college. Your father and I will get you some counseling. You can stay at home as long as necessary."

"Don't blame yourself, Mom. I got myself in this trouble, and Dalvin and I will figure it out. But I'm not coming home. I'm grown. Things aren't as bad as they seem. I don't live in this tent. We use it to sell drugs. The police assume we're homeless, which allows us to get away with what we're doing. The school said they wouldn't press charges."

Not blaming myself is easier said than done. What would people think of Richard and me once this gets around? Remembering I'm in a location where drugs are sold, I peek outside; anyone could shoot up the place. What have we walked into? Is Dalvin human trafficking Gerolyn?

"So, Dalvin is the name of the man I need to kill. Where is he?" Richard says. "What did he say to get you so gone in the head? He must've taken your virginity. Whatever you have going on with him is over." He stands to leave. "We're not going without you. If I must carry you out, so be it."

That's right, Richard, take charge. She is still a minor, and I don't care if she's a college or ex-college student. She is our baby, even if Dalvin is pimping her out and took her virginity. We'd return the car rental, buy her an airplane ticket, and return to the Midwest, where she'll enroll in a new college and get a fresh start. This will have all been a nightmare we'd soon forget.

"There's more. It gets worse," says Gerolyn. "You'll soon understand why leaving isn't an option. You all may never want anything to do with me again."

What does she mean? Nothing is worse than selling drugs. I can only pray to Mother Mary for direction and brace myself for disaster. Gerolyn has yet to get to the life-or-death matter. I don't know if I can handle it. Everything in me wants to shake her, but I must keep it together. She'll shut down and run back into Dalvin's arms if I go off, and I may never see her again.

"Spit it out. Whatever it is, me and your mother will manage." The glance Richard shoots at me makes me wonder if he trusts I could cope. He has a right to doubt me. I'm crumbling on the inside, struggling to keep a poker face. "If Dalvin or his people have threatened you, tell us. We'll get you out of here and contact the police once we get home. He won't be able to hurt you. Does he know our home address?"

"Listen to your father, sweetie." *Prove to me you aren't an idiot*, is what I want to say.

"No one threatened me. We're in love and will be a family one day. If it were only the drugs, I wouldn't have involved you all. I've gotten good at selling. I'm living with Dalvin and his family until we get our place. Someone's life is on the line; that's why I called."

She's ruining her life for some boy me and Richard haven't even met. Love. What does she know about it? We sheltered her. Our families told us she'd grow up and rebel. I'm responsible for my child getting kicked out of college and likely on her way to prison.

"Dalvin and I needed money bad. We're saving for an apartment in West Hollywood, and it's expensive. And I don't need to tell you how much planning for a wedding costs."

She must be kidding. We are in a tent, the school kicked her out, and she's considering marriage. She's seventeen, for Christ's sake.

"Try not to judge me for what I'll say next. There was this rich girl on campus who thought she was better than everyone. Her parents are loaded and donate to many things at the school. Dalvin and I kidnapped her a week ago."

"You did what!" Richard yells. "Who are you, and where is our child? Kidnapping. Drugs. Are you trying to destroy your life? Are you on drugs?"

"Gerolyn, baby. What has that boy done to you?" I remove my phone from my purse and begin dialing the police. A part of me is pleased that Gerolyn knows she can trust us. She still thinks because we're her parents, we know everything. The truth is, I don't know how to handle any of this, and I doubt Richard does. The police would know what to do.

Charging me, she snatches the phone from my hand. "I know you lost your damn mind," I say, taking back my phone. She'd never done anything disrespectful like this.

Richard steps between us, and good he does since I'm seconds from slapping common sense into her.

"I'm sorry, Mom. If we involve the police, the girl we kidnapped will be killed. She's in a house not far from here, and Dalvin's cousins are watching her. Her parents refuse to send the ransom, so Dalvin wants to kill her. One of his cousins and I voted to let her go, while the other agreed with Dalvin. Dalvin says she'll tell if we release her."

"Where's Dalvin?" asks Richard, for a second time since Gerolyn failed to answer previously. When she ignores him again, Richard's speech becomes pressured, as if he wants her to see how serious things are. "If we call the police, the problem will be solved. We'll say that as soon as he told you he kidnapped the girl, you called us, and we flew here to help because you were scared Dalvin would kill you if you involved the police."

We could save our daughter if only she'll allow it. Even though she is wrong, she's still our blood. I'd die before I let her ruin her life, and I'm certain Richard feels the same. Maybe I can say something to convince her to see things our way. "Whoever that girl is, I'm sure her parents are worried. I'd be if it were you. You know better than this. Think, Gerolyn."

"No police!" she yells, wide-eyed, trying to assert her dominance. "Dalvin went out of town four days ago to handle business, but we haven't heard from him. He's not answering his phone. That's why I called you. I need to figure out what to do to save the girl and avoid prison."

"Take us to her," I say. "Perhaps if your dad and I talk to the kidnappers, we can convince them to let her go." On the other hand, we all could be killed, but I don't say this aloud. My instinct is to protect Gerolyn, but I couldn't live with myself if I didn't help that other girl. I have no weapons but trust Archangel Michael to protect my family.

"How many men are at the house?" asks Richard. "Do they know we're here, and do they have guns?"

Shame covers Gerolyn's face; she is staring at the ground again. She should be ashamed. The morals we instilled are now non-existent. "There are two guys. The one who thinks we should let the girl go knows you are here; the other does not. Since Dalvin isn't answering our calls, I might be able to talk the one who disagrees with me into letting her go. She's adamant she won't tell anyone. Dalvin took the guns with him. All he left us with are machetes."

I'm not street smart, yet I have seen enough TV to know the kidnapped person always promises not to tell. This proves how dumb my child is. Dalvin figured out their plan wasn't well thought out and left his cousins and Gerolyn to take the blame.

"I hope you see Dalvin doesn't love you. If he did, you wouldn't be here alone." I pray she lets my words sink in. Although Richard and I argued in front of her when she was growing up, more than I care to admit, we didn't teach her struggle love.

The frown on her face shows my words went in one ear and out the other. "He loves me. Something must've happened to him. He'll be back for me. You'll see."

"We need to go," Richard says. "Take us to the house so we can reason with Dalvin's cousins. We'll figure this out on the way."

Gerolyn leads us out of the tent, and I can't stop looking around me. Who knows if someone will try to rob or kill Gerolyn, assuming she has drugs on her. The police could have gotten word of the drugs and are watching Gerolyn. I don't feel safe here. Yet, I doubt I'll feel better at our next destination. If Gerolyn was the only one involved in the kidnapping, I could take charge, but she's not. Now, outside of the rental car, Gerolyn insists on driving her car while we follow her in the rental. Having no choice but to let her take the lead, we hesitantly go along.

INSIDE THE CAR, I try comprehending where I went wrong as a mother. If I had let her spend the night at a friend's house or stay out later, she wouldn't have turned out this way. We required her to attend church, respect elders, and do well in school. I thought we had done right by her, but today proves we dropped the ball. "Hail Mary, Full of Grace, the Lord is with thee," I pray aloud to comfort myself.

Ruining my moment, Richard says, "Mary won't help. What would've helped is if you had attended the generational curse breaker church conference. The ministers led us in prayer to break ancestral curses. While I broke every curse on my side of the family, you stayed home, pretending to be sick. You missed out on breaking the generational curses on your side of the family. Whatever Gerolyn is going through is because of your genetics."

As if I wasn't racking my brain enough, he laid this burden all at my feet. "Don't start. We need to be united. Who knows what we're going to walk in on? Neither of us has ever dealt with this, and either those boys or the police might kill us. You want to spend what could be our last days on earth blaming me?"

"You don't want to hear the truth. Your brother got into a shootout with the police and provoked them to kill him. That's suicide. Your mother always calls saying she has dreams of us dying or something bad happening, and it never does. She has anxiety issues she refuses to deal with. There's no mental illness on my side of the family. Gerolyn is struggling with her mental health. Why else would her personality change drastically?"

Everything he said about my family is true. However, his family, too, has issues. Just because they don't struggle with mental illness doesn't make them better than my family. "You should've prayed away the evil spirits in my family while you were at the conference. What sense does it make to pray away spirits on your side of the family and not do the same for mine? You do realize we're one flesh. You're selfish. Gerolyn got some good sex and has lost her mind. That's all this is about. We're both to blame. The purity until marriage talk that you had with her before college backfired." I don't believe my family is plagued with demonic spirits, but I'm tired of hearing Richard talk. If I push back, maybe he'll shut his mouth. My plan works; he turns up his gospel music to drown me out. So much for coming up with a game plan.

Twenty minutes later, Richard parks across the street from Gerolyn on a residential street. When we exit the car, I invite my family into a huddle on the sidewalk. I'm not going into that house without some idea of what to expect. Will Dalvin's cousin turn on us? Hell, they might take us hostage, assuming we have money. Gerolyn is dumb and probably told them how much Richard and I make a year. I say another prayer for boldness because I'm anything but in this moment. "We should call the cops in case Dalvin comes back. Gerolyn, you said he has guns."

"He'll never hurt you or Dad. Worst-case scenario, if he refuses to let the girl go, I'll stay behind. You two go home. If the police catch us, I'll say you all came here on vacation and knew nothing about what I had going on."

"They won't believe that," says Richard. "You're coming with us after we wrap up here."

Gerolyn walks off, dismissing Richard. Had this been under any other situation, I'd point out I don't like how rude she's acting toward her father. "Come with me into the house," she says. "I'm sure his cousins will listen to reason and let the girl go. She'll keep her mouth shut. We've been feeding and bathing her. We took her against her will, but we've treated her good."

My poor child has lost her mind. She believes Dalvin cares about her and that he'll spare us. If I asked, she wouldn't be able to name one kidnapped person who didn't run to the police after getting free. Gerolyn's soul would be lost if we didn't get her away from Dalvin; she's already lost her cheeriness and innocence. I wish I could go back to the days when social anxiety was her only concern. Damn, Dalvin. If I see him, I'll strangle him and don't care if he shoots me. My once meek daughter is gone, and it's his fault.

We follow Gerolyn to a pink one-story house where the grass is freshly cut, flowers bloom, and a welcome mat is in front of the door. The property looks like it belongs to a loving family who cares about its upkeep. If this is the headquarters for where Dalvin's family sells drugs, no one from the outside would know. Certainly, the neighbors wouldn't suspect a kidnapped victim is inside. Someone's child is being held against her will, and it's Gerolyn's fault.

"Whose house is this?" I ask, inhaling the aroma of grilled meat coming from the house. Something is off. Gerolyn can't cook; perhaps Dalvin's cousins cooked. How did they find the time to grill when they have a kidnapped victim? Further evidence they and Dalvin are amoral.

"We'll get into that later, Mom." That wasn't the response I was looking for. If I must fight, claw, or chew my way out of the house, I'd do it to save my family. I'm not letting Richard carry the burden alone. If one dies, all die.

When I get inside, the first thing I'll do is search for weapons. I might have to kill everyone who's already in the house, except the victim.

After Gerolyn unlocks the door, Richard moves her to the side and enters first, and I'm impressed that he wants to ensure our safety. When we enter, a room full of people shout, "Surprise!"

"What's going on?" I ask Gerolyn, relieved we didn't walk in on Dalvin's cousins murdering the girl. Richard and I look to one another for answers, but when we realize we're both clueless, we turn to Gerolyn, who might be experiencing a mental break. She's giving us a goofy look as if she's scared to fill us in. After everything she's shared today, I can't imagine she'd be scared to tell us anything.

As I wait for her to say something, I examine my surroundings. There are balloons, flowers, food, and presents everywhere. We walked into a celebration instead of a crime scene with machetes. Everyone looks happy to see us, but Richard and I are anything but excited.

Gerolyn laughs nervously. "I got you! Surprise! I was joking about everything. I didn't get kicked out of school, I'm not dealing drugs, and no one was kidnapped. I paid someone to use their tent, and I dressed like I rolled out of bed before coming to you all to cause concern."

"Why would you scare us like this?" Richard is glaring at Gerolyn like he wants to put her over his knee and spank her. The room of people would get a cheer from me if he snatched Gerolyn up. "Had us come all the way to Los Angeles, and nothing is wrong."

The partygoers, whom neither Richard nor I know, are listening to our conversation and likely thinking our family drama is better than any movie. "Gerolyn, answer us. What's the meaning of this?" I ask, tired of the suspense.

Rather than answer, she yells, "Dalvin, come from the kitchen."

Dalvin is real. I still don't want to meet him. Had he put my child up to this? Whatever this is.

An average-height, thin young man comes around the corner and hands me flowers, and I accept. He attempts to shake Richard's hand, but Richard refuses. Dalvin says, "I'm happy to meet you and excited you two are here. I'm sure you have a lot of questions, and we'll answer them all."

"You better." Richard takes a step toward Dalvin and gets in his face. I haven't seen Richard this angry since he got road rage and tailgated a man last year.

"Mom and Dad, me and Dalvin are five months pregnant. This is our baby shower. I didn't know how else to tell you because I knew you'd be disappointed. In one of my classes, I read a book about a guy who wrote a letter to his parents, telling them he dropped out of school to become a male prostitute, and shortly after, he developed HIV and had only a few months to live. His parents were devastated. The guy then told them that it all had been lies, and the truth was he had gotten an F in a class and was nervous about telling them. Once they discovered he wasn't dying, they couldn't care less about the failing grade. "Do you all forgive me?"

Richard and I hug her, and I say, "Of course we forgive you." I think I speak for Richard when I say we absolutely don't forgive her.

Not long after, I'm on the couch next to Richard, trying to enjoy myself, but it's hard. I'm relieved Gerolyn is safe, hasn't kidnapped anyone, and is still in college, but she's too young to be a mother. Doing something this extreme to tell us about my grandchild shows she has much to learn. If not for the guests, Richard might've had to hold me back from strangling Gerolyn. Instead, we play nicely, getting to know Dalvin, his family, and Dalvin and Gerolyn's friends. Dalvin is a smart young man who is doing well in college, yet my motherly instincts scream to drag Gerolyn and my grandbaby back to Indianapolis so I can take care of them both. I don't bother mentioning my concerns to Gerolyn, who can't keep her eyes off Dalvin, who looks at her with the same intensity.

Resting my head on Richard's arm, he caresses me, and I imagine he's pretending to be happy while thinking of the money he spent on the last-minute flights.

The End

new year, new me... now what?

. . .

EVERY WEEKDAY, I stand in my local coffee shop, eyeing a well-dressed, handsome man and wishing he was mine. His eyes never linger on me like mine do his body, but I'm enamored with him, nonetheless. His suits fit him well, and the watch on his wrist shines brightly. He must have an expensive tailor or a girlfriend at home who makes sure he's immaculate and looking as if he's going to walk the runway. What I wouldn't do to have someone like him. I'd settle for someone who looks half as decent. Because of my looks, I don't ask him out, even though he buys me a caramel macchiato whenever I'm fortunate to be in line behind him. He purchases everyone's drink in the line, meaning I'm not special. He believes in paying it forward, which would be the only reason he buys strangers' drinks. I always thank him and get annoyed that I don't say more. Horace is my crush's name, and he's kind to everyone he comes across: he remembers the cashiers' names, leaves hefty tips, and smiles and chats with everyone except me.

Today, as I stand behind him, I look at myself in my compact mirror while pretending I'm scrolling on my phone. I want to ensure I look decent, even if Horace wouldn't know if I was dead or alive. I've put on a few pounds over the years and am the biggest I've ever been, but

I'm not hideous. When he pays for my order, I thank him and quickly avert eye contact. Men can tell when a woman likes them, and I don't want him to know my secret. Not yet.

While waiting for my order, I stand a few feet from Horace so he doesn't think I'm stalking him. A much bolder woman approaches him, and seconds later, she walks away, looking defeated. Horace doesn't wear a ring, so he must be in a committed relationship. Men like him are never single. The women who strike up conversations with him all look the same: thin with hair down their backs—some with weaves, and others with natural hair. I run my fingers through my shoulder-length blow-out, wondering if I got another hairstyle, would he be interested? Who am I kidding? It's not my hair turning him off, it's the weight.

I stop thinking about Horace once he grabs his usual order: a large iced green tea. Each week, I tell myself I'll order a healthier drink to be more like Horace, but I never do. When Horace passes me, he smiles. I turn my head, knowing the smile must be for someone else. I'm right. To the side of me is an eager-looking woman waving at Horace, and he's waving back. It's not the first time I thought he was happy to see me, but he wasn't.

I told my good friend, Talese, about him, and she said I should ask him out. What do I have to lose? My dignity is what I'm afraid of losing, but I didn't share this with Talese. Men in my league never make me shy, but Horace is out of my league. Something about his outgoing personality and ability to chat with anyone stops me from saying hello. He carries a briefcase and sometimes takes business calls inside the coffee shop. He's someone special at work. I imagine he's the CEO of his company, and he started with little to no help. He has employees vying for his attention, and he never had anyone refuse him a contract.

One day, when I lose weight and get a new job, I'll get the courage to talk to him. I'm on leave from work because of a nasty fall. My ankle is taking longer to heal than expected, and my doctor says it's because of my weight. I can walk on it, but it hurts.

HOURS LATER, I'm at the doctor's office, waiting for the doctor to enter my room. When the door opens, I say, "Dr. Francis, I need you to refer me for gastric bypass surgery." Her giggle throws me off. I'm serious, and she's laughing. "What's funny?"

"You're overweight, Amya, not obese. And you don't have health problems. I'll gladly schedule an appointment with the nutritionist, and in no time, if you eat healthily and exercise, the weight will come off."

This is why I dislike primary care physicians. They are unnecessary hurdles on my path. I wish my insurance allowed me to see any doctor of my choosing rather than begging the primary care physician to grant me a referral. I stand and lift my shirt, revealing my large stomach, stretch marks, and back rolls. Perhaps seeing what I'm working with will convince her to help me rather than going by some stupid BMI chart. She turns her head like she's offended, further proof she might not be the doctor for me. It shouldn't be shocking to see a stomach. Instead of calling her out on her unprofessionalism, I say, "You scheduled me with the nutritionist last year. Remember?" Her expression says she hasn't a clue what I'm talking about.

Now that my shirt is down, she makes eye contact with me. "How did that go?"

Apparently, it didn't go well if I'm sitting here asking for bariatric surgery. But instead, I say, "I didn't go. Something came up," I lie and then feel bad, so I confess. Growing up, my grandmother shamed me when catching me in lies. Since she passed, I have strived to be honest with everyone to make my grandmother proud. I like to imagine she's giving me a thumbs-up from heaven. "I didn't feel like it. I need something that works quickly. My life is passing me by, and nothing I do to lose weight is working. I used to like skating, but with the weight, I'm too tired to do it."

"You can't skate anyway with that ankle of yours." That wasn't the point. Before the ankle injury, I stopped skating. "How can you say nothing works when you haven't visited the nutritionist?" She flips through my chart after making her snarky comment and then notes something. I bet she's writing that I'm a difficult patient because I have the audacity to advocate for myself. When I extend my neck to see what she's writing, she stares at me like she has caught me misbehaving.

Doctors think they know it all. However, this is my body, and I know what's best for it. "It's not as if I can't find whatever the nutritionist has to say online. Seeing one is a waste of time. What I can't do for myself is the surgery. That's where you come in." It was time to remind her why I'm here. She's not leading this conversation, I am. Most doctors have God complexes and are used to patients acquiescing, but I'm not that patient.

"What other things have you tried to lose weight?" She pulls up a chair and leans into me like she cares.

Although I want the interrogation to end, I humble myself and answer. She has something I need, after all. "I've gone to the gym and have eaten healthy, and I'm still fat."

Her list of follow-up questions keep coming. Why does it matter how long I tried exercising and eating healthy before I quit? She denies the referral and put in yet another request for me to see the nutritionist. As a final slap in the face, she reminds me that my insurance pays for a local gym membership. What a waste of time. I bet she'd give me the referral if I had better insurance.

AFTER LEAVING the doctor's office, I lay on my sofa, talking to Talese, who I suspect gets tired of me complaining, but that's what friends are for. I fill her in on my visit to the doctor. "American doctors are a waste of time. How will I ever be bathing suit ready and looking good for Horace if I don't get surgery? I don't have the energy to exercise or eat lettuce all day. Once I get the surgery, I'll be motivated to live healthier."

Sounding like my doctor, Talese says, "If you can't live healthy now, who's to say you'll be successful after the surgery? People claim they'll do all sorts of things if only, but seldom mean it."

This isn't the support I'm looking for. Everyone doubting me makes me feel like a loser. "What other people do and say has nothing to do with me. Let's change the subject. You don't understand."

"You're annoyed, but it's a valid question. Promise you'll think about what I said. You don't need surgery, especially not to please a man. One you've never spoken a full sentence to. If you show interest, he might ask you out."

Easy for her to say I don't need surgery. She has never had a weight problem and assumes it's easy to lose fat if I weren't lazy. I might not be super fat, but I'm big, nonetheless. And she has a man, so I don't care what she says about Horace. If he were into me, he would've let it be known by now. I am done talking about me. "How was your day? Is your boss still picking on you?"

"Amya, I can't stand you sometimes. You only want me to agree with you. When I don't, you change the subject."

"It's not like that at all. I just want what I want, and I'm tired of others questioning me about it."

"Lucky for you, I love you and might be able to help. Why are you saying 'hmm mmm' before I finish speaking? You can be negative sometimes." I want her to say what she has to say so we can move on. She probably has some diet and exercise plan she wants me to follow. I'm not going on a raw fruit or smoothie diet. Been there and done that. "I shouldn't tell you what I'm about to, but I know how persistent you can be. You won't stop telling me about that surgery until you find someone to do it. I don't want anything bad to happen to you. My cousin got gastric bypass surgery in Mexico and paid out of pocket. The girl ain't dead, so I'd count it as a success. She had problems only after overeating, but I hear that's to be expected. I could give you her number. At least I'd know you might come out of it alive."

Now, this is unexpected information. Finally, someone is helping me. I have money saved, so I could get the procedure sooner rather than later. If I need more money, my parents will loan it to me if I lie about why I need it. Grandmother won't be happy, but this is a special situation. The last thing I want is my parents to bombard me with questions and worry. I put them through so much when I was younger; I avoid stressing them now.

For a few years, I hung out with a wild group of girls; we carried knives and stayed in trouble. I did things that disappointed my parents and others close to me at the time. My parents and others in authority always tell me I go too far. However, I have no regrets; I never started anything with anyone. My decisions got me placed in juvenile hall and the hospital, but I'm stronger because of my past.

After the call, Talese texts me her cousin's information, and I reach out to the cousin, who answers all my questions. The surgery is not as expensive as I assumed, so I don't have to bother my parents. With the help of a language translation service, I call the Mexican doctor and make my appointment, which is a few weeks away. Perfect timing. By the new year, I'll be more confident, look better, and have the confidence to approach Horace.

Back on the phone with Talese, I update her, and she hesitantly agrees to come to Mexico with me after I inform her the clinic won't do the surgery if I'm alone, for safety reasons. I don't know what I'd do without her support. We'll arrive a few days early and go sightseeing.

"Amya, are you sure this is what you want? It's not too late to cancel."

"I know you mean well, but this is my life. Yes, I'm sure." When she drops the subject, I'm relieved. I can't be too upset because if she were the one getting cosmetic surgery, I'd be afraid for her too.

THE DAY before Talese and I leave for Mexico, I'm back in the coffee shop, checking out Horace from behind, wondering how many squats he does at the gym. The way his muscles bulge out of his suit jacket makes me imagine the gym staff having to throw Horace out at closing time. Why can't I have his willpower?

As is our routine, Horace smiles after paying for my drink, and I thank him. This time, I order a large green tea. I'm already making healthier choices; I only wish I didn't add two sugars. While I'm wiping up the sugar I spilled on the counter, Horace stands to the side of me, staring at me. Something must be wrong with me. My hair must be out of place. He won't stop looking, which makes me self-conscious. I muster the confidence to ask, "What's up?" I'm dumb. After months of seeing him, 'What's up?' is the best I could come up with.

"I always see you here, but we've never said more than a few words to one another." He introduces himself, and I pretend not to know his name before telling him mine. "Do you work nearby?" I gaze up at him in disbelief this moment is happening. He's probably questioning what's taking me so long to respond.

Finally, my mouth becomes unglued, and I say, "I live up the street. You work around here?" I'm able to have an adult conversation, after all.

"My office is a few buildings over."

"Convenient. Well, I gotta go. Nice meeting you." From the looks of it, he might've been on the verge of saying something as I walked off and out the door. But I have to go because the other women are giving me the mean girl eye because they think I'm not good enough. And they're right. Horace only talked to me to make me feel less awkward about spilling sugar on the counter. He felt sorry for me. Or he had great sex this morning and thought he'd strike up a conversation with the woman no one else in the coffee shop pays attention to.

TIME FLEW BY, and Talese and I are now in Mexico City. For the last couple of days, we did our sightseeing during the day, ensuring we were back at the hotel before dark since Talese heard about Americans going missing. I'm not worried about human traffickers or someone assaulting us. Since I was a teen, I carried knives in my purse, and I can take a punch. I couldn't bring my favorite blade to Mexico, but when room service delivered our food, I stole the knife for protection. I've never seen Talese fight and doubt her skills since she wears long, manicured nails, prefers heels, and talks often about women not being gentle enough. She doesn't know much about my past because I only share enough not to seem closed off. People have preconceived notions about former gang members; I want to be judged on who I am today: a law-abiding citizen.

Today is the day of my surgery, and while waiting in the clinic waiting room, out of nowhere, Talese says, "Are you sure about this? Just because we're in Mexico doesn't mean you have to go through with the surgery. Don't do this for someone else. If you must go through with it, do it for you."

"As I said before, I know what I'm doing. Horace is one of the reasons I'm doing this, but not the only one. I'll advance in my career, and who knows what other doors will open for me. I'm tired of people judging me based on my body before they get to know me."

"Don't you think you're a little too into him?"

It annoys me that she won't say what she feels rather than questioning me. "I think you should be my friend and support me." I hold back yelling at her. Now isn't the time to put doubt in my mind. I should be relaxing to prepare myself for what is coming. People want to hear what they want. She brought up Horace but pretended not to hear my other reasons for the surgery. It's not like I'm obsessed with him. As soon as a woman shows ongoing interest in a man, others make her feel bad. Talese should be glad I'm not the person who complains and does nothing about it. I don't like my size, singleness, or my job. So, I'm taking steps to change.

After seeing that I couldn't be talked out of the surgery, Talese backs off and practices her broken Spanish with staff and the others in the waiting room. Most of the staff don't speak English, which would be scary, if not for Talese helping me communicate.

Now, on the operating table, I visualize how I see my life after surgery. My ankle will heal faster, and I'll be back to skating and might check out some dance classes. I'll have the confidence to apply for management roles at my place of employment. None of the supervisors look like me. All of them are fit, which leads me to believe that only thin people are promoted. Each time I walk into the office, I'm aware I'm different. My mood is lifting, thinking of the possibilities for my soon-to-be thin self.

Currently, I use my vehicle to drive clients who struggle with substance abuse to and from appointments and other places they want to go. I hate the job, but it pays the bills. What makes me most excited is the number one reason I'm doing the surgery—Horace. If he has a girlfriend, I'll date someone else until he becomes single. I might look so good that I'll meet another man and soon forget about Horace, but I doubt it.

Interrupting my thoughts, the doctor and his staff enter the room, and they're ready to put me under. Not long after, I zone out, anxious to awaken a new woman.

After waking from surgery, it feels good seeing Talese's face, proving I'm alive. I'm in pain, but not hurting as much as I had imagined. Not long after, the doctor gives me new information but claims he told me and Talese on the phone before I got here. Since I doubt that he's lying, I blame Talese's ghetto Spanish. He tells me that upon my release, I must go for walks, although I'll be in pain, to release the oxygen he pumped my body with. Thankfully, he gives me painkillers.

The following days, Talese supports me while I walk the perimeter of the hotel. Whenever I want to give up, I remember Horace and get motivated to release oxygen from my body. People look at us with questioning eyes, but I'm on a mission, and don't let it bother me.

DAYS LATER, we make it back to the States, and I hire the nurse who helped Talese's cousin after her surgery. This icky tube hanging out of my stomach needs cleaning often. I try cleaning it on my own but am freaked out, knowing the tube is attached to my stomach. I hope Horace appreciates all I'm doing for him. It's for me, too, but he's my biggest motivator.

When I can't sleep because of pain, I remind myself why I got the surgery. Horace. I often sit in bed, thinking about how I'll ask him out. Where he'll take me. Even though I'll pursue him, I want him to take the lead and plan a date—even pay for it. I bet he enjoys plays and musicals. Something tells me he's a man with high-class taste. I don't care for such entertainment, but I'll keep an open mind for him. Everything about him screams money, which works in my favor. Since Mexico, I'm too low on funds to take him out.

When I tell my parents what I've done, they're disappointed, which is to be expected. Anything could've happened to me, they say. Although I tell them Talese was with me and would've called if anything went wrong, it doesn't make them feel better. Like my American doctor, they don't think I needed the surgery, and I should've put more effort into diet and exercising. If those things alone worked, we wouldn't have so many overweight Americans. My parents mean well, but what do they know? Both are fat, and if what they're telling me works, they would've made it happen for themselves. Hell, I blame them for being overweight. The only reason I confessed to them is the pain is so bad I couldn't keep it between myself, Talese, and the nurse. When I'm suffering, everyone needs to know.

Weeks have passed, and I haven't returned to work. My ankle continues to hurt; therefore, the physical therapist hasn't cleared me. I'm barely eating and drinking because, when I do, I feel stuffed. The only thing I drink with ease is Ensure. When I'm around my parents, I want to eat what they have, but I can't. I haven't returned to the coffee shop and miss Horace. I've lost weight; I can feel it. I refuse to weigh myself since the number on the scale can be traumatizing. My clothes fit loose, which is a sign the surgery worked. I had hoped my clothes wouldn't fit at all by this time. Thankfully, Talese has been great at reminding me to be patient.

On the New Year, I bring it in with my parents. My appetite is better, but I don't force myself to eat, or I'll become sick. I've spent enough time away from Horace and the coffee shop; let me return before he forgets me.

IT'S JANUARY 2ND, and I'm feeling great. A new year, a new me. I'm ready for love. I get my hair and nails done and buy a new outfit. No one can tell me I'm not beautiful. Men are looking at me in a way they never have before. I avoid eye contact because I only have eyes for one man.

Hours later, I'm at the coffee shop, and nothing has changed except for my transformed physique. Horace is ahead of me in line, looking fine as usual. He buys everyone's drinks, and I get a small green tea since my new stomach can't handle a large. When I step out of line, I approach Horace. I'm everything he's looking for in a woman: beautiful and thin. I don't need a pep talk; I'm most men's dream these days. I could lose a few more pounds, but Horace will see the new me and realize I'm a work in progress. I have some loose skin under my sweater, but it's well concealed with a tummy holder.

Horace is leaning against the wall, texting, but I don't let that stop me. I interrupt. "It's been a long time since I've seen you." I look him over. "I love you in that suit." It's one I haven't seen him in before. Navy blue suits him well. His stylist or woman deserves a thank you. Someone knows about skin color and complementary colors.

He's looking me up and down and looks dissatisfied. "You look different, Amya," he says dryly and emotionless. Am I misreading his expression?

Horace remembers my name. My excitement fades when he doesn't smile. "I've been hitting the gym to get in shape. Health is wealth," I lie, hoping Grandmother is busy enjoying heaven and not paying attention to me now. He stays in the gym, so I want to show we have things in common.

"Mmm, okay," are his only words.

Where is the cheery Horace who grins at every woman who starts a conversation with him? My ego is crushed. I'd prepared to ask him out but hoped he'd beat me to it. I've had too many painful, sleepless nights to get scared and abort my mission. "I never see your girlfriend here with you. Why is that?"

This gets a smile out of him, and I'm hopeful. "I'm single. Since last year, I have been building the courage to ask you out. I told myself I'd finally do it this year." Yes! Yes! Dreams do come true. "You always seemed so shy when I tried getting your attention. I didn't think you were into me, so I never asked for your number."

Am I hearing him correctly? The times I thought he was smiling at me, there were always other women around. How had I missed the clues? The important thing is that we both want each other and are both single. A year from now, we'll be engaged and planning our wedding. In two years, I'll be pregnant, and we'll be moving from a condo to a house to prepare for our growing family. Life is good. Something tells me this year will be the best so far. Let me not get ahead of myself. "I like you," I say. "I assumed you had your eye on the other women who are always all over you. I'm glad we cleared this up." I pull out my phone. "I'm sure you need to get to work, so let's exchange numbers. I can't wait to learn all about you."

It seems as if he's struggling to find words. What's the hold-up? He places his phone in his suit jacket. Maybe he didn't hear me, so I ask for his number again.

"I hate to be rude, but I'm no longer interested." This isn't what I expected to hear. He places a comforting hand on my shoulder because my mouth is open. "I don't mean to offend, but I like big women. You were everything I wanted in a woman." I'm not liking this conversation at all. I cut my body for him. "You're too small for me. I like a woman whose back rolls I can grab." He stares out the window at the snow and then turns to me. "It's cold outside. I need a big woman I can cuddle with on the couch and drink hot cocoa with."

He can't be serious. Had he told me he liked me fat, I would have stayed that way. Is he playing games? "I'm confused about your liking big women. I always see model-looking chicks around you, and you seem happy to talk to them."

"You see them approaching me, but never me going after them. I've never exchanged phone numbers with any of them. I'm kind because that's who I am. They aren't my type, but I don't have to be rude."

When he pulls out his phone, I assume he has changed his mind about me, but I am wrong. He shows me pictures of him with past girl-friends. All are fatter than I once was and gorgeous. Never would I think they'd be his type.

He looks up from his phone. "As long as you're happy with yourself, that's all that matters. You'll find someone who loves you for you." Sensuously, he licks his lips. "Forgive me. I was fantasizing about how you used to look. I'll see you around." He exits the coffee shop, leaving me dumbfounded. I can't believe he thinks treating people like this is okay. He's dismissive instead of rewarding me for taking control of my life.

Outside, ahead of me, posted against the coffee shop, is Horace and a woman twice my size whose face he's smiling in, telling her how beautiful she is. Either he doesn't notice me or couldn't care less I'm overhearing their conversation. I had assumed he was a good man, but he proved me wrong.

He's busy scrolling on his phone, preparing to get her number, I imagine. Little does he know, he's broken my heart and has rewarded my kindness with evil. He's no different from the girls who bothered me back in the day and assumed I wouldn't get up with them. Everyone always assumed I was nice until I surprised them. I'm a kind person until provoked. Now, in front of Horace, I startle him when I throw my drink in his face. This small act of aggression makes me feel a little better. As if I'm in the wrong, he's yelling and saying something is wrong with me. The woman scowls at me while using the napkins in her hand to help Horace dry himself. When I pull my blade from my purse, the woman is the first to see it. Speechless, she walks backward with her hands in surrender. Good for her to realize this isn't what she wants. This is between Horace and me.

Unfortunately, Horace doesn't see the blade until I swing it across his high cheekbone. Now I feel good since we both have cuts on our body. He should endure pain as I have had to. The woman screams while Horace is bent over, holding his face. His blood makes the snow look like a cherry-flavored snow cone. A few nearby people cover their mouths, and others point at me while I leave the scene on my way home. They probably assume I'm the bad guy, but they'd be wrong. Whenever the authorities catch up with me, they, too, will blame me for what I did to Horace. I haven't been to Hamilton Psychiatric Facility since I was a teenager, and I suspect I'll end up there again or in jail. However, facing consequences for my actions doesn't bother me as much as having to find a new coffee shop.

The End

if you're reading this letter

. . .

DRIVING to the bridge where I plan to kill myself, I can't stop thinking about my family. Too bad I won't be around when they read the letters I left behind. I take pleasure in knowing they'll blame themselves for my decision. They'll reflect on what they could've done differently to save me. The course of their lives will never be the same, thanks to me. That's what they deserve: pain. Just like they gave it, they should feel it. I've always been good to them, and for that, they rewarded me with indifference.

When I get to La Muerta Bridge, a place some locals go to commit suicide, I'll jump off and onto the freeway. Guns are too violent. I'd have an anxiety attack thinking how painful it would be to put a bullet in my head, and I wouldn't know how to get my hands on a gun. I guess if I walk the streets of Hollywood, I'd find someone who could get me one, but that's risky. Someone might call the police. Hanging myself also came to mind, but I wouldn't want to be found with a broken neck. Gruesome. Jumping off the bridge seems peaceful. I'd say goodbye to the blue sky, stare at the clouds, and smog one last time before my body crashed into the cars below. It'll be wild to see cars scrambling to get out of the way to avoid hitting me. Life has been hard; I don't care about traumatizing anyone else. My dramatic death will only serve to bring more shame to my family. If I died at home, they and their friends would cover it up and tell people I died from a medical condition. Being splattered on the freeway leaves no room for deceit. Like good old Dad, I'll make the paper and be a star. He says I don't apply myself enough and I'll die a no name. I'll show him.

I park my car in a residential area and walk a block to La Muerta Bridge. Minutes later, I'm leaning against the railings, peeking over at the oncoming traffic that's moving fast. Do I really want to do this? My senses are overwhelmed. The noise coming from the traffic makes it hard to think. I imagine the blow of cars hitting me and the pain I'll endure before death. I hate pain. Am I ready for my bones to break against the asphalt? I didn't come this far to back out. I'm no coward. Dad always tells me I must live boldly.

A car passes me. I pace the sidewalk to avoid bringing attention to myself. If someone alerts the cops that I'm looking over the bridge, I'll end up at Hamilton Psychiatric Facility up the street. I'm not nuts; I don't belong there.

Committing suicide should be a right for every citizen. It's my body, and I should be able to do with it what I please. That doesn't make me crazy; it means I'm taking my destiny into my own hands. A girl who looks close in age to me is approaching. She appears sad underneath her baseball cap. Her eyes are glued to the ground, and her shoulders are slumped. She might be here for the same reason as me. To my surprise, she stops in front of me, smiles and introduces herself. Although I'm not in the mood to talk, I tell her I'm John. I'm expecting her to move on. Instead, she talks to me about what's viral on social media. I don't add much to the conversation and don't tell her to get lost. It couldn't hurt to have one last conversation with Ella before I take my life.

"What brings you out here to creepy La Muerta Bridge?" Ella asks me, knowingly, and I don't like that she assumes she knows what I'm up to.

I lie, "I'm out for a walk. How about you?" I don't trust her. Because of the increased rate of suicides at this location, she could be working undercover with the police to stop suicides. I might be making too much of this. Would the police have an undercover suicide task force?

"Like yourself, I'm enjoying this beautiful, sunny day. I come here to think."

"What a strange place to come think." I say, "There are so many other places in the city with a better view. The beach. Griffith Observatory."

She points her finger into my chest. "What a strange place to go for a walk, John. You don't look like you live around here. At least I've never seen you."

What does she mean, I don't belong? I glance at my clothes, and unlike her, who is dressed in shorts and a top revealing her belly button, I'm wearing pressed slacks and a button-down shirt. I want to look good on my death day. People wouldn't have as much sympathy for me had I dressed down. They'd assume I was a meth head who gave up on life. I tell Ella the truth because what could it hurt? "I don't live near here, but the beauty of having a car is I can go anywhere I want." She's weird, but I have some time before I work up the nerve to jump, so I'll get to know her. "Tell me about yourself."

Ella reveals she's a struggling college student who lives in an apartment not far from here. She failed her exam and came here to sulk. Her boyfriend is an asshole, but she loves him. Although she enjoys the city, she's conflicted because her boyfriend wants her to move back to Texas with him once they graduate next year. To show interest, I grunt, nod, and ask follow-up questions. Mother always tells me how self-centered I am, but what does she know? Ella is convinced I care since she keeps talking. I don't, but I'm good at pretending.

After talking my ear off, she asks, "How come you want to die?" She stares at the sky and twirls as if to say life is wonderful.

She reaches her hands out for me to twirl with her, but I pass. Why couldn't I be as happy as she now appears? What happened to the sad girl? It's strange how she knows what I'm here for. Do I look depressed? Should I confess? I have nothing to lose. If she runs off and snitches, I'll be dead before help arrives.

"Are you psychic? Or are you projecting? Maybe it's you who wants to kill herself."

When a stranger passes, Ella moves out of the way and sits close to me on the railing like we're the best of friends.

"I've been told I have psychic energy. But I can't figure out why you want to off yourself. You look like you come from money and have everything you need. Your clothes are name-brand, you have a fresh haircut, and your cologne smells expensive. Someone either loves you, or you love yourself way too much to jump."

Her assumptions about me are off. Of course, I look good; Dad has money. But that doesn't mean I love myself or that I'm loved. What does it mean to love oneself? This world is cruel, and I've had enough. Escaping my life will take the pressure off me. I won't have to decide what to do for my future, and I'll no longer hear my parents arguing. I'm only twenty, and my family thinks I should have my life together and be a better role model for my sixteen-year-old brother. I'll teach Ella a lesson about not judging a book by its cover. "You think you have me figured out, but you don't. I, too, hurt. I'm going to kill myself, and don't try to stop me." There's a look of surprise on her face; I suspect she didn't think I'd own up to my plan. I've been told I'm truthful to a fault.

"You don't have to worry about me trying to stop you." She leans in and gives me the most intense stare. "All I ask is that you prove to me your life is so horrible you should kill yourself. After all, I'll be the last person to see you alive. People will want to know what you said to me before you jumped, and if I'm going to get my fifteen minutes of fame, I want to sound intelligent. You wouldn't want me telling reporters I know nothing."

"No one will know you were here if you leave now and leave me to it."

"That's not true. At least one person has walked past and seen us together, and numerous cars on the freeway have driven by. A witness will say they saw two people sitting on the rails before the guy took his life. Tell me why your privileged life is so bad, and I'll be on my way."

The sarcasm in her last sentence makes me want to justify myself. My dad is in the entertainment industry, and people always make assumptions about me, assuming I have it good and want for nothing. Just because I live in a wealthy neighborhood and have everything I want means little to me. When you're raised around money, it doesn't impress you. All I want to be is loved and my parents failed me.

I remove folded letters from my pocket and hand them to her. "These are copies of the suicide letters I left for my so-called loved ones."

She pushes them back into my hands. "Read them to me. It won't be the same if I read them. I want to feel the intensity behind your words. Whatever you said in those letters had better convince me you should die."

If I believed in God, I'd think He sent her to stop me from doing what needs to be done. She sure is pushy, but I'm convinced I'll win her to my side once she hears what my family has done to me. Something inside me screams not to open up to her about sensitive family matters. I'm not afraid of crying in her presence. I just don't know if I want her to critique me. I'll listen to her input to be kind, but I'll kill myself anyway. Only I know what's best for me. She couldn't possibly advise me after only meeting me minutes ago.

To get her out of my hair, I read the letter I wrote to my dad, whom I'm named after. "If you're reading this letter, it means I'm dead. People will tell you not to blame yourself, but they'll be wrong. You're at fault.

"All my life, I have wanted you to spend time with me, yet you were too busy. Either you were on set, shooting a movie, traveling the world, promoting movies, partying, or out cheating on Mom with other women. Of course, you'll say you attended networking parties, but you always came home late and drunk afterward. How much networking were you doing? I can hear you justifying yourself, saying you left me at home with Mom. Let me tell you what you conveniently forget, Dad. Mom was depressed and anxious and not much for company."

I pause and glance at Ella, who seems unconvinced that I have a reason to kill myself. She signals me to continue. A part of me doesn't want to because she shouldn't matter to me. Another part wants someone, even if a stranger, to know how rough I've had it. "What kind of father hires a male babysitter to babysit his sons? A father who cares about himself, that's who. I never told you this, but Trevor used to make me suck him off. I did it because he'd threaten to tell you and Mom lies about me if I didn't. Trevor would make me get undressed and touch himself. Thankfully, he never touched me, but he scarred me, nonetheless.

"Mom was good-for-nothing back then and now. She'd be in the room, down the hall, and none the wiser to what was happening under her roof. Trevor was your friend's son, so the blame falls at your feet.

"One day, I had prepared to confide in you. I worked up the courage and couldn't sleep the night before. You had promised to come to my baseball game and take me out to eat afterward. I was going to tell you then because it would be just you and me, but like always, you missed that game. I had to live with the secret. I'd think either you or Mom would notice the difference in me after Trevor began taking advantage of me. When my grades dropped and I lost all motivation, you both accused me of laziness. No one asked why I was jumpy whenever Trevor came around or why I, as a ten-year-old, cried when I was left with him. You idiots didn't think it strange. May the rest of your life be worse than the life I've lived." Holding back tears, I hurt for my younger self, who was alone.

I look at Ella and am pleased with the look of empathy on her face.

"I'm sorry that happened to you," says Ella, rubbing my arm so gently I resist the urge to lay my head on her shoulder. "Your parents should've protected you, and they didn't. If he's still alive, expose Trevor. Don't let him get away with this. You shouldn't kill yourself because he was a creep."

Her touch continues to soothe me, which is why I don't complain when she rubs my back. I like that she's understanding. I have no one who cares to listen. Friends only use me for loans they never pay back. They want to be bothered with me, hoping that my father will bring the latest 'A' list celebrity around and they can get pictures to post on Instagram.

"I don't want anything to do with Trevor. He'll be like all other pedophiles who deny what they've done. Plus, my parents have the suicide letter with his name, and the letter will be on me when I die. Trevor will get his in the end. I'd be too ashamed to be alive while others knew I was molested. It's embarrassing. You understand?" Then it dawns on me that Ella is the only person who knows what happened to me, and I'm not ashamed. I don't know what to make of this. Perhaps I could handle exposing Trevor. To stop myself from screaming at the thought of Trevor, I read the note I wrote to my mother.

"Dear Mom, whoever told you it was a good idea for you to have kids was wrong. Over the years, I hoped you would get better at mothering, but you failed at every turn. After you saw that you were trash, you had the audacity to get pregnant again. Your only redeeming quality is stopping after kid number two.

"If you're reading this letter, I'm dead. I've thrown myself off a bridge because of your horrible parenting. We have loads of money, but you never enrolled in an alcohol rehab. It makes no sense. Did you think I couldn't smell alcohol on your breath? You'd be in the bed sleep while I was giving Trevor head. He took advantage because he knew you didn't care about me. Had you, you would've been aware of what was going on inside your house. I could excuse you, had you had a job and come home tired and crashed in your bed.

"The nights when Dad wasn't home, you made me snuggle with you in your bed until I was eleven years old. Do you care how uncomfortable that made me feel? Although you never did any freaky stuff with me, I felt violated. No boy wants his drunk mother sobbing on him and telling him about his father's many whores. Whenever you were halfway sober, you'd remind me how good I had it. Good how? The times you didn't forget about my baseball games, you showed up drunk, wearing too much makeup, and dressed like you were going to a movie premiere. You're a sorry excuse for a mother. All my friends laughed at you and shook their heads at me. I hate you. If there's a hell, do me a favor and rot in it. Sincerely, your son who killed himself because you ain't shit."

Ella's tears confuse me. We only met today, so she shouldn't cry for me. I don't want her to feel sorry for me, only to understand why I'm doing it. It's important she does not think I'm crazy and belong in the mental hospital.

Turning her back to me, she wipes her tears and faces me. I already saw her crying. Maybe she turned her back to me because she's not the sensitive type. She could've fooled me, the way she's been rubbing me. There's something motherly about this girl.

"Life can be hard. Your parents didn't have it in them to love you as they should have. But trust me, if you kill yourself, they'll go on with their lives. They'll mourn you for a while, yet they'll get over you. Your brother will have kids, and they'll take joy in being the best grandparents possible. Soon, your name will be mentioned less and less. You'll be a dark part of their past they force themselves to forget. They have money, and they'll probably start a foundation in your name, and people will sympathize with them, not blame them. And since they don't care like you say they don't, you know I'm right. Don't hurt yourself to get back at them. It'll only backfire, and you'll be dead-maggot meat."

"You really think they'll move on with their lives and forget about how bad they've treated me?" Ella can't be right. No parent wants their child to die before them. They'll suffer for the rest of their lives.

Cars pass in front of us, so Ella speaks up so I can hear her. "People are more resilient than you give them credit. Your mother buries her head in liquor, so she might be too drunk to process what happened. If you assume your family's life will derail because of you, you might be a narcissist.

"I had a cousin kill himself, hoping to make the family feel bad. Everyone did for a few weeks, but then life returned to normal. Bills were due. Other problems arose. My cousin was soon forgotten.

"At first, the family celebrated his birthday each year, but even that stopped. I still love him, but I don't think about him as much as I did when he died." I'm taking it all in. I've never known someone who killed themselves. Ella speaks with confidence, like she knows what she's talking about. I nod, letting her know I'm considering what she's saying. "The best thing you can do is do something with your life and get away from your family. You're young and good-looking. Whatever you want to do is available to you. If you don't seize your opportunities, you're a failure and can't blame it on your family." Ella stands in my face and places an 'L' for loser on her forehead, which makes me laugh, something I haven't done in weeks.

Knowing my family, Ella might be on to something. They'd tell everyone I was suffering from a mental illness, and they tried to get me help, but I refused. It would all be lies, but my dad's publicist would come up with something tragic yet believable that places my parents in a good light. I look over my shoulder at the traffic underneath that continues to move at a fast pace. I won't tell Ella about wanting to make others pay by causing a car crash. She might not think well of me, and though I don't know her well, I like her and care about how she feels about me. If I cause another's death, I'm no better than my parents. This girl is getting into my head. "I'm listening, but I haven't made up my mind. You've given me some things to think about."

To my surprise, Ella, who's still in front of me, shakes my shoulders. Startled, I brace myself to prevent myself from falling over the railing into the traffic. "Boo!" she says, smiling. About what? I don't know.

"What did you do that for?" I stand and get in her face to scare her, although I'd never hit a girl. "You could've killed me."

Unbothered by the fake tough guy persona, she motions for me to sit and joins me. Cautiously, I do, but I keep my eyes on her in case she makes any more sudden moves. "For someone who wants to die, you sure dug your feet into the concrete and held onto the railing for dear life a second ago. John, I won't think poorly of you if you've changed your mind." My instincts had kicked in since I wasn't expecting her to play around. It doesn't mean I want to live. When I look at her like she's annoying, rather than answer her, she says, "Go ahead and read your other letter and do better this time at convincing me."

I read my last letter addressed to my brother Phil to paint a full picture of my horrible family. "I used to like you when you were younger, but you let our parents get into your head and poison you against me. Sad. You're in high school, and things are going well. All the girls like you, the boys want to be you, and the scouts are already looking at you. I can't lie; you're one hell of a baseball player, but none of that makes you better than me. I'm the one who taught you to play. Remember, Dad was too busy.

"These days, we don't talk, and it's not because I don't try. We pass one another in the house and don't speak. All you do is shake your head at me like I'm a loser. I don't like it. Only if you knew why I'm not a better role model, never had a job, or enrolled in college after barely graduating high school. Trevor, our babysitter while growing up, molested me. I allowed it because I was scared. He threatened me, and part of me wondered if he'd come after you if I didn't give in to his desires.

"I was right about him not touching you; had he, your life would have been drastically different. You aren't screwed up because you haven't faced what I have. For that, you should thank me. Mom and Dad never showed you much attention either, but I did. Where they failed you, I did my best to make sure you were good. Did you forget all I've done for you? When Mom was drunk, which was more times than not, she burnt our eggs and toast. I learned to cook so you'd have digestible food each day. When our parents forgot to get groceries, I learned to shop and use their credit cards to make sure you were okay. They could never remember to sign your field trip or sports permission slips. Had it not been for me forging their signatures, you might not be in sports today or so well-rounded. Then, to have you grow up and look down on me, that hurt. I desired more motivation, but it didn't desire me. I love you even if you don't love me. I want Mom and Dad to suffer for how they treated me, but I hope you'll reflect on our relationship so you can be a better person by learning to appreciate those who love you." I finish and can't wait to hear what Ella thinks. I'm sure I convinced her I should die.

"How do you feel about everything now?" Ella asks, looking up at me like she hopes I've changed my mind.

That's a good question. I still want my parents to suffer and be humiliated. Taking my life might make Phil a better person. All I've ever wanted was for him to smile at me and adore me the way he did when he was much younger. Another benefit of death is I wouldn't have to think about my future: finding a girlfriend, looking for a job, or starting a family. No one talks about the stress of adulting. I could get a regular job, but my father's fans will always compare me to him and say I'm a loser. Phil has no plans to become an actor, but he has what it takes to make it to the baseball league and become well-known in his own right. What do I have? Nothing.

"Leave, Ella. The only thing you've accomplished by having me read the letters is reminding me why I'm at La Muerta Bridge." I stare over the railing at the moving cars. "Get the hell out of here unless you want to see me kill myself. I don't want this on your conscience unless you're into creepy shit." I climb over the railing and am facing traffic. I begin counting in my head. Once I reach one hundred, I'll jump, whether Ella is here or not. She's been warned.

"Wait! I have a secret to tell you." I suspect she'll tell me she, too, is here to kill herself. I wouldn't be shocked since she was sad when she first approached me, and crying when I read my letter was strange. This chick is depressed. It had never crossed my mind to kill myself with a partner, but I'm down if she is.

Ella unzips her purse and removes a hunting knife. I put distance between us to protect myself if she lunges at me. If I'm not careful on the railing, then I'm roadkill. I'm suicidal, but I don't want to die because I slipped. Or because Ella bludgeoned me.

Cars beneath me are blowing, and some change lanes. The noise is unbearable. I should jump, but I promised myself I'd count to one hundred first. A part of me wants to know what Ella has to say, so I listen to her. "Don't be mad, but I knew who you were when I introduced myself. I brought this knife to kill you."

Her sudden revelation makes me desire more distance between us. Who is she? Why does she want to kill me? I seldom leave my home. I haven't done anything to anyone, at least not that I know of. Has she been following me? Or is she a serial killer who befriends and then kills random strangers?

"Are you nuts?"

She chuckles, letting me know I'm on to something. This girl is crazy. She comes closer so she doesn't have to shout over the traffic noise. I never take my eyes off the knife. "Calm down. I changed my mind after getting to know you." To put me at ease, she throws the knife onto the freeway. Now that she no longer poses a threat, I swing my legs around the railing. "I'll tell you why I've been following you." I look her up and down to see if she has more weapons. When I tell her I don't trust her, she opens her purse, and it's free of weapons. I'll throw her off the bridge if she pulls a weapon out of her pockets. "You don't know my mother, Faye, but she used to sleep with our father back in the day." She pauses and stares at me. I'm assuming I have a look of disbelief on my face. "Hear me out. It'll add up in a bit. Because my mother didn't like condoms, she got pregnant with me. Our good old dad left me and my mother eventually, and she never went after him for child support. She thought of herself as an independent woman. Stop frowning. I can prove it." From her purse, she pulls out a picture of a woman and my dad holding a baby girl on his lap. Even though I dislike Dad, I got territorial when Ella called him her dad for some reason.

"Why do you want to kill me? My dad is a ho, not me. I didn't know you existed until today." I have the worst luck. How is it I come to La Muerta Bridge to kill myself and meet Ella, who wants me dead? Or wanted me dead? I don't know what to believe.

"I assumed you and Phil had perfect lives. Our dad stopped coming around when I was seven. As I got older, I began following him online and was jealous when he posted pictures of your family. It was easy to find his address. I pretended to be a tourist and went on a Hollywood Tour bus ride since they're known for riding past famous people's homes. Sure enough, we passed dear dad's house. Soon after, I began driving past the house, watching who came and went. I knew your name and what you looked like from pictures online. Today isn't the only time I followed you, but it's the first I got the courage to kill you. Never would I have imagined you were coming here to kill yourself. I parked down the street not far from where you parked."

Her words baffle me. She looked distraught when we met; I assumed she was having a bad day. All along, she was working up the nerve to take me out. To kill someone with a knife is bold. "When you told me about your horrific life, I realized I didn't have it so bad after all. Me and Mom were poor and struggled more after Dad disappeared. She got cancer, and I had to live with relatives for years. They didn't want me around and made sure I knew it. My mom pulled through, though, but died last month."

The caring part of me wants to touch Ella's knee when she tears up about her mom, but I don't since I'm unsure how it'll be received. Knowing the reason she's here also stops me from comforting her. "I promised myself I'd get revenge on our dad. I blame him for all the problems that happened after he left. But now I see I was lucky not to have him around. He hates you as much as he does me."

She pulls out more pictures, and I look at them. When she showed me the first picture of her as a baby, I was uncertain whether the child was her. Growing up in the spotlight, I learned not to trust people. She could've gotten that photo from anywhere. Dad might've posed with a fan and her child. But undeniable are the pictures of him lying shirtless in a bed with a woman and him playing with someone I recognize as a young Ella. Dad's a known cock hound in the entertainment world, and now I see it for myself.

Everything in me wants to help guide Ella through life since Dad abandoned her and her mother. I'm not the one who wronged her, but I feel responsible. It's weird, but I'd like to get to know her. I wonder how many people she has in this world besides her boyfriend. Maybe I could stay alive a while longer to ensure she's good. I might kill myself in the future, just not today.

"I'm sorry about your mom and how our dad treated you." It feels like slow motion when I place my hand on her knee, and she covers my hand with hers. Her acceptance of me means the world. "You're right. You are better off without him. Phil isn't that great, either. He reminds me of our dad, so you might not like him if you were to meet him. You were really going to kill me?" I'm looking at her and don't think she has it in her to take a life.

She pretends to slice her throat. "You were as good as dead. I figured if I took Dad's firstborn, his pride and joy, it would be the ulti-mate revenge. After telling you that people don't care about us as much as we think, it dawned on me that harming you to hurt Dad wouldn't be a good enough punishment. If he has an ounce of love for you, he will get over your death."

Wow! The seriousness of her tone and facial expression convinces me she would've killed me. I've never met anyone like her. Now that we've cleared the air, I'm willing to move forward. "I have an idea. Come home with me to meet the family. I can't wait to watch them squirm."

"I like how you think, brother. I'm in. I promise I won't kill anyone.

Is it okay if I call you brother? I'm an only child and always wanted siblings. What will you tell them about the suicide letters?"

"I'd like it if you call me brother. I doubt they found my letters; no one has called or texted. Even if they find them before I get home, after I introduce you, the focus will be on Dad's cheating and you, his love child. Mom knows he's unfaithful, but I doubt she knows about you. Who knows how many kids he has around the world? I thought I'd be rich after his death, but I might have to split my inheritance with a tribe."

"We could kill any sibling who shows up after me." She says she's kidding, and I believe her.

"Is your name really Ella? And how old are you? You don't look like an Ella."

She laughs. "It's Jasmine, and I'm nineteen. I made up the story about the boyfriend, but everything I said about my mother is true." She's one year younger than me. Dad should be ashamed that he couldn't keep it in his pants. "I lied in case you survived the knife attack. Once, I cut an ex-boyfriend who hit me, and it landed me a week at Hamilton Psychiatric Facility."

"I'll be sure not to get on your bad side." I should be scared, but I'm not. Though I don't know her well, I'm confident she's what I've been missing. Oddly, I feel closer to her than anyone in my life. Too bad it took nearly killing myself to find her. My sister and I hold hands while heading to our cars. The family get-together will be one to remember.

The End

crappy grandmammy

. . .

I SIT on the edge of my bed, pulling up my stockings over my hairy legs and getting ready for church. When I was a worldly woman, people couldn't pay me to wear stockings or not shave my legs. Since Jesus, my life has changed for the better. If all He requires of me is to look holy, the least I could do is comply. He died for me on the cross, so having itching legs during church service won't kill me. To think, He gave His life for someone like me who used to be in the streets drinking, smoking, having sex, and gambling. It's cringeworthy thinking of the vile lifestyle I once lived, but that's the old me. My daughter keeps bringing up my past to make me feel bad, but I try not to let her drag me down. I can't blame her for not knowing how good Jesus is. How he picked me up, washed me, and made me whole. I let my light shine daily, hoping to save a few family members and other sinners.

From my bedroom, I hear my family arguing above the blaring secular music. They know I don't like worldly music, especially not on Sundays. As the head of the house, they should listen to me, yet that's not the case. Every night at bedtime, I pray that the Lord saves my family. He hasn't done it yet, but I'm patient.

After dressing, I follow the smell of bacon to the kitchen. "Praise the Lord," I say to my thirty-year-old daughter, Katina, and her boyfriend, Quintus, who are eating at the table. I had her when I was sixteen, and she's been a thorn in my side for more years than I'd like to count. After living with me for years, there's no sign of her leaving. Guilt keeps me from throwing her out.

"Good morning, Grandmammy." Katina laughs at the greeting she gives me, although there's nothing funny. I blame Jashaun for her calling me this name; he's her sixteen-year-old son who used to call me Nana until watching some movie where a boy referred to his grandmother as Grandmammy. No matter how many times I've asked him and Katina to stop calling me Grandmammy, my protests have gone ignored. Perhaps it's acceptable in some cultures to call a grandmother Grandmammy, but not in mine. It's disrespectful, and I want it to stop. That word makes me feel much older than I am, as if I'm on my way to the grave. My breasts no longer sit up as they once did, and menopause hasn't been kind to me. The last thing I need is more reminders that I'm getting old; the mirror never lets me forget.

Quintus throws a sausage at Katina, and I chuckle when it bounces off her head and onto the floor.

"That's what you get for not honoring me, Katina," I say. "Roll your eyes all you want. You know it's true." One day, Katina and I will have a good relationship, but from the glare she's giving me, it won't be today. If only she could let the past stay in the past.

"Stop disrespecting your mother. You rude as hell." I appreciate Quintus coming to my defense; however, he disrespects me too. Even though I tell him he can't sleep here, he does it anyway. Katina and he think I'm stupid. Quintus leaves the front door open at night, and when I go to bed, Katina lets him back in. I'd protest, but Katina would lie and say I'm imagining things. However, I'm aware Quintus wakes early each day, gets out of Katina's bed, comes downstairs, and pretends he just arrived.

Refusing to be humbled, Katina grabs a handful of eggs and slings them at Quintus. As he wipes his face, Katina stands and yells, "Don't get in between family business. You weren't there all the nights I cried myself to sleep at my grandmother's house because Lisha was in the streets." Her calling me by my first name is disrespectful. I gave birth to her, after all. If I didn't think I could save her, I'd put her out of my house.

"Grow up." Quintus slams his fist against the table.

I'm not worried about him harming her; he's not that kind of person. Still, I can't stand to hear pointless arguing. To gain control, I say, "Enough. This is God's day. Katina, turn that music off. I shouldn't have to shout in my own house."

After she begrudgingly obeys me, I go to make me a plate. Of course, Katina didn't think enough about me to make me some food. Every day, I have high hopes for her, and she lets me down. I must take some blame for our relationship. Hoping to make her feel bad, I say, "I guess I have to fix food for myself." I pull out eggs and sausage from the refrigerator and then slam pots against the stove. "If I stopped making Sunday dinner, I bet people would be upset."

"Are you saying something, Grandmammy?" Katina is trying my nerves, pretending she doesn't know I'm talking to her and Quintus. My attempt to guilt her fails again.

I ignore her comment because my spirit will be negative at church if I don't. God has done too much for me not to praise Him. I look inside the sink, and the roast I told Katina to take out of the freezer earlier this morning isn't soaking. If I didn't do things myself, they wouldn't get done. No one appreciates me, and I do so much for them. "Why didn't you take the roast out of the freezer, girl?" I wait for her to get defensive rather than admit her mistake.

As predicted, she says, "I got a lot of stuff on my mind. Why didn't you do it yourself? I told you that Quintus and I are going out later. We might not be here to eat the food, anyway, so why would I care if you ate? Jashaun might not be here, either." Jashaun was at Katina's father's house this weekend. I wonder if he refers to his grandfather as Grandpappy. If he does, I've never heard him. It's not right, but if the boy disrespects me, he should disrespect his grandfather too.

"I knew I couldn't count on you. I'll do it myself." When I approach the freezer, Quintus jumps up, pulls out the roast, and soaks it. After thanking him, I make my food and sit at the table to eat. With the sight in front of me, I'm surprised I can keep my food down. Katina is in

Quintus' lap, kissing and rubbing on him like I'm not here. Quintus pulls away when he sees I'm staring.

"Why you stop kissing me, daddy?" I don't like the look Katina gives me after Quintus nods his head toward me. "Don't worry about her. She used to have men around me all the time. She acts holier-than-thou, but you should've met Lisha back in the day." She tongue kisses Quintus and then winks at me in defiance. "We ain't doing nothing but reminding her who she really is. Those church lady clothes are hiding a heathen. Heathens never reform." She looks at me, daring me to object.

My mother practically raised my kids. I was a baby myself when I had Katina. There was so much going on in the hood that I couldn't be bothered being a full-time mother. Back then, I had so much energy I couldn't sit still and always knew where the party was, what liquor store had the cheapest liquor, and where to get the best drugs. Attempting to control me, my mother punished and threatened me, but I had a mind of my own. I'd sneak out of windows and not come home until the morning. Judgmental people used to tell my mother that something was wrong with me in the head. At the time, I assumed they were old, bitter, and wanted to be young like me. When I consider my life before the Lord, those people may have been on to something. I had problems.

Despite the bad things I did as a young mother, I made sure Katina was taken care of. My mother lived on a fixed income; she could barely provide for me and my siblings, let alone Katina. I was home every morning to get Katina prepared for school. If I didn't pick her up when the bell rang, I would pay someone to do it. I wasn't the homework-helping kind of parent, and I don't feel guilty about it. The teachers got paid to teach and do homework; that wasn't my job. I regret not hugging her more, asking about her day, and being too busy to take her to birthday parties. Even though she had every toy she wanted, nothing could make up for me not being there consistently. Her father was heavily involved in her life, but a girl needs her mother.

I beat myself up over some of the stuff I didn't do, but as the pastor says, "God has forgiven you, so why not forgive yourself?" Instead of justifying myself to Katina, who is rubbing on Quintus like she's ready to undress him, I change the subject and remind her what's important. "Today is the fifth of the month, and you haven't given me the rent money, and I need it before I go to church."

She pulls the money from her bra and slides it to me. I haven't seen a woman do this since my mother passed away. Katina is like my mother in many ways; both enjoy arguing and hearing themselves talk.

I count the money, but it's not adding up. "You're forty dollars short." I charge her four hundred dollars a month, which is not bad for her, Jashaun, and Quintus. She could at least pay what I ask. Contributing to groceries but not helping with anything else is manipulative. The people at church say I should put her out; one of these days, I'll listen. When I think of telling her to leave, I ask myself what Jesus would do. What if something bad happens to her in the streets, and she's not saved? She'll go to hell, and her blood will be on my hands. If she's here, I can mold her. She pretends she's not listening, but I know some of what I say sinks in.

"You're the one who said I could move in so you could be closer to Jashaun. I did as you asked, and now you're complaining about forty dollars." She waves me away like I'm nothing.

Her memory is conveniently wrong. After Katina called last year saying she was getting evicted after losing her job, I told her she could stay with me for a time. We never discussed how long she'd live here. That was my fault. I told her I wanted her and my grandson here rather than couch surfing at Katina's friend's house.

I'm responsible for how she turned out. When pregnant with her, I smoked weed and drank; that's why she's slow today. Her father was dumb too. Back in the day, the local hood boys paid him to go to the corner store for them. They couldn't go for themselves because they had beef with gang members who frequented the same store. Katina's father wasn't in a gang and was liked by people in various hoods, which is why he could go to the store and not get killed. People called him a flunky behind his back, which he was.

One night, I was horny, and Katina's father was the only person around, so I settled on him. When I had sexual desires, they had to be quenched immediately. Something was wrong with me, but I don't know what. No one molested me. I just felt good when a man was on top of me or cuddling with me. However, I was so easy that not many stayed around long enough to spoon. To my dismay, I got pregnant. Two years later, I got pregnant by him again, but I miscarried. What can I say? The store runner was always available, and the sex was good. He's a good father and now an even better grandfather, but seldom deals with Katina because of her smart mouth.

Before I can demand my money from Katina, Quintus hands me sixty dollars. "Don't worry about it, Ms. Lisha." I thank him, and then Katina argues about him giving me the money and an extra twenty.

It's time to leave for church, but I can't go without extending an invite like I do every Sunday. "How long will you two play with God? Come to church and give your lives to the Lord."

"You know better than to ask me that," Katina says. "You had better not give my money to that pimp you call a preacher." One day, someone will stop Katina from running that mouth of hers.

"Someday I'll come to the Lord," says Quintus, looking uncomfortable with the conversation.

"What makes you certain you have another day on this earth? Today might be your last to let God in your heart." Ignoring me, he buries his face into Katina's body. I give up and go to the living room, where I grab my purse and keys and walk out the door.

Inside my car, I'm rifling through my purse when there's a knock on my window. I roll down the window to talk to Jashaun. His grandfather blows, waves, and pulls off. Perhaps Jashaun wants to go to church with me, but he's dressed in jeans, and I know he doesn't think he's coming with me to the house of the Lord dressed like this.

"You look pretty," he says. I stare at my plain white blouse and white skirt that hit my ankles. I look like I'm wearing a tablecloth, so he's lying and wants something. "Say a prayer for me. You got some money I can have? Me and my friends want to get pizza later."

I know all too well Satan himself lives behind that smile. Katina poisoned Jashaun against me. Even though I'm against fornication, I want Katina to have more kids so I'll have a fresh start at being a grandmother. If Katina keeps living with me, I can ensure the new baby thinks well of me. My chances with Jashaun are bleak since he's set in his ways. "I don't have any money for you. Go talk to your mother. She cheated me out of forty dollars. And why are you going out to eat? I'm cooking the roast when I get home." Maybe I'm harsh. I know what it's like to be a kid and not want to eat homemade food.

Before I can apologize, he says, "That's okay, Grandmammy. I know you're poor and need the money more than me." While he approaches the house, I pray to God, asking Him to intervene in my and my family's lives. Jashaun yells over his shoulder, "Bye, Grandmammy." The old me wants to curse Jashaun out. Jesus, take the wheel.

WHEN CHURCH BEGINS, I can barely listen. I keep asking God when will my family love me like I love them. I don't get an answer, but something tells me that whatever word the visiting minister delivers will be from the Lord's mouth.

An hour later, I'm singing praise and worship, and my spirit has lifted. No longer are my family problems weighing me down. The praise team takes their seats when the pastor comes to the pulpit and introduces the guest minister. Not long into the message, I'm pleased that the message is indeed for me.

The guest minister, who is well in age, says, "I don't mean to be harsh, but God ain't happy with some of you. You've taken Him for granted, and all He asks is that you be fishers of men. You must do better at winning souls. Why are there so few people here this morning? How do you have people living in your homes, and they're still not saved? That's a reflection on you. Are you letting your light shine? Or are you drinking and smoking with them? Have you convinced them that hell fire is hot, and once in it, no one can pull them out, not even God himself? Wake up, people of God. Do better. The next time I come, I want this place packed with your family and friends."

There are a few amens, but many keep silent. I suppose, like me, they feel guilty. The minister's words are tight but right, as my mother used to say. I haven't done enough to get my family on the Lord's side. I thought inviting them to church made me a good Christian; I was wrong. I continue listening to the minister to learn how to win my family over.

"Get in their faces!" the minister shouts. "Tell them to accept the Lord or get out of your house. Don't go to their get-togethers if the Lord isn't the center of the conversation. You know your family better than me. Think what it would take to make them say yes to Jesus. For my daughter, it was putting her out at eighteen to experience the harshness of the world." He waves at his daughter, who is much older now, and she waves back. "You all see she's here with me, serving the Lord today. Some family members you must stop talking to or stop giving them money. They want your listening ear and your finances, but not your God. That's not right."

Service is almost over, and I know now what I need to do. The Holy Spirit gives me instructions. I'm honored He'd visit a former sinner like me. The minister is correct; I know my family better than anyone. Yet, anything I come up with to save them won't make them repent. The Holy Spirit's idea is risky, and I question it, but He's convincing me the word came from the Lord. How can I protest?

Before leaving the church, I shake the minister's hand to thank him. I'm dissatisfied with myself for second-guessing the Holy Spirit, but I desire confirmation that what He said is correct. I don't want to mess around and do something, assuming it was the Lord's will. I must be in the will of God. "The Bible says we must be harsh with some people to save them from hell. Right?" I ask the minister since he knows the word better than me.

"Indeed, it does, sister. Something tells me that a nice lady like yourself is too easy on your unsaved loved ones. Toughen up, sister." His encouragement is what I need to follow through on my instructions.

NOT LONG AFTER, I enter my home, and everyone is in the living room. I hand Jashaun money to buy pizza, drinks, and snacks for him and his friends. I don't have money to spare, but I must be alone with Katina and Quintus. At sixteen, Jashaun hasn't reached the age of accountability; he has time to consider if he wants to live for Jesus. Quintus and Katina must decide today. Once Jashaun leaves, I stand in front of the TV.

"What are you doing?" asks Katina, snapping at me as if I'm not her mother. She doesn't even talk to Jashaun the way she does to me. "You ain't been home five minutes and bothering us. The roast is thawed. Go cook and make yourself useful."

I haven't put my purse down or taken off my stockings, but I have a mission that can't wait. "You two have seen me serve God for years, but neither of you have moved to accept the Father and the Son. Choose today who you'll serve." The confused looks Katina and Quintus give one another doesn't deter me. "Who will it be? Satan or Jesus. Choose wisely." I've never been this direct with them, but I have to say it like the Holy Spirit told me.

"I'm gonna go, Ms. Lisha." Quintus stands, not comprehending the seriousness of the decision he must make. "I forgot I had some things to take care of." Little does he know that God's mercy might no longer be available for him, depending on his answer. Since Quintus has been around for years, I consider him family. He'll get the same treatment as Katina. I pull my gun from my purse and aim it at him. Finally, I feel in charge. My gun goes everywhere with me. I did unspeakable things when I was in the streets, and I never know if someone from my past wants to harm me.

"Grandmammy, what the hell are you doing?" She stands to approach me as if I'm not holding a gun. And has the unmitigated gall to call me grandmammy at such a time. "I thought you got rid of Betsy." Betsy is the name of my gun. The last time Katina saw it was when she was in high school. We were in line at the store, and a man cut in front of me and cursed me out when I said something to him. When Betsy came out, that fool got to apologizing so I didn't have to shoot him. Had it not been for his change in tune, I would've gone to jail that day. "I don't know what sermon they preached today, but you better stop playing."

I aim the gun at her to show I'm standing on business, as Jashaun says. "Sit your rude self down and hear me out. You never listen, but today you will."

"Ms. Lisha, put the gun away. What's up with you? This ain't like you."

"Sit. Both of you. I won't say it again." This could be easy or hard. The decision is theirs. Quintus obeys. Smart man. But Katina moves closer to me, and I shoot a hole in the ceiling to grab their attention. She backs off, showing she's not that slow. They both look scared, but I don't know why. I'm not asking them to do algebra; all I've given them is a simple decision to make. "Will you all accept the Lord or not?"

Katina and Quintus call me crazy, but many people of God have been called worse. "Who will be your savior? Satan or Jesus? It's my last time asking." Why can't they do the right thing? Don't they know how good life with God could be?

"I ain't accepting nothing!" yells Katina. "Grandmammy, you're threatening us and think we want your God. You belong in a mental institution." She laughs. "You better get that gun out of our faces. Or…" It hurts to do it, but I shoot her in the face. I love her, but I love Jesus more. The sight of her is horrific, and tears roll down my face. Who would've thought I'd be the one to lay my only child down? Her father will be angry and hate me; however, he doesn't know the Lord, so his opinion doesn't count.

Before I can say a prayer over Katina's body, Quintus runs toward the door. Out of compassion, I advise him to stop. He forces my hand. When he touches the doorknob, I shoot him in the back, and he staggers. Determined, he turns the doorknob, but it's locked. I must save his soul. "Who do you want to serve?" When he hits the ground, his eyes are wide. He's not moving. He's dead. I feel bad they didn't make the right choice, but I tried working with them.

After asking God to have mercy on their souls, I gather clothes, set them on fire, and scatter the clothes around my home. A cleansing is needed. Who knows how much fornicating has happened in my house? Everyone except me played un-Godly music. Everything in my home has been tainted. I need a fresh start. Jashaun will miss his mother. Hopefully, someday, he will understand why I did what I did. He might be better off without her. Katina wasn't all bad as a mother, but she should've taught Jashaun to respect me and forced him to come to church.

Exiting my smoky house with my phone, I dance on the lawn while listening to my favorite church song, "Stomp" by Kirk Franklin. The devil thought he'd put me in hell for not converting my family; I fooled him. Praising God uncontrollably is my way of celebrating that heaven is my destination. The flames coming from the house grow out of control. I'm so unfazed that I ignore the neighbors who pull me from the yard when I don't leave willingly. Not even the sounds of fire trucks stop me from worshiping. I'm so into my favorite song that I have on repeat that, like King David, I strip out of my clothes and run up and down the street until officers tackle me. I'm assuming they aren't saved. Or they would've known what I'm doing is normal for a believer.

WEEKS LATER, I'm at the Hamilton Psychiatric Facility, where un-Godly professionals and police keep asking why I did what I did. They say Jashaun had a psychotic breakdown and is now in the same facility on the children's floor. That can't be true because I asked the blood of Jesus to cover him and keep him safe right before the officers tackled me the day I danced naked for my Savior. Satan's children are lying. The staff and police will say anything to make me talk.

When my pastor or any of the people of God visit, I'll tell them my story. I've been waiting a while for the body of Christ to visit, but they're taking longer than expected. I'm sure they haven't forgotten about me. True believers will find me relatable. Non-chosen ones won't comprehend the assignment the Lord gave me. A perfect example of why I don't talk is a rude staff member who checks on me most nights and often asks how I can sleep, considering what I've done. My response is always the same: a laugh. If she mattered, I'd tell her that I sleep like a baby every night because the Holy Spirit whispers to me, "Well done. My good and faithful servant."

The End

he hurt me. how could he?

. . .

PULLING up to where I live, I turn off the car and hope to sleep well tonight. I stare up at the apartment buildings, wishing I lived there. People don't appreciate what they have until it's gone. This won't be my life forever. Eventually, I'll bounce back on my feet. I don't know whether this is true or something I tell myself and my unborn child to make us both feel better. Staring at my stomach, I rub my belly and encourage my child, Shannon, that we will be okay. We won't be homeless forever. I promise her we won't end up like me and my momma, living in every homeless shelter in the city. Although I'm struggling, I won't have us in a shelter getting bitten by bedbugs or dealing with rude staff who look down on us.

Shannon kicks. I want to think it's because she trusts me, but maybe she senses how stressed I am, and she wants me to stop lying to her. After cracking the windows to ensure we don't suffocate during the night, I put on the window sun blockers, although it's nighttime, to avoid people seeing inside my car. This is a good neighborhood near a community college but the students are nosey. Last night, someone yelled inside the car, saying the police were coming. Scared, I pulled off. After driving aimlessly for a half hour, I returned to my normal resting spot and went to sleep. It was dumb of me to believe I would be in trouble. A month ago, someone called the police, and once the officer discovered I was fine, he left. I'd heard stories of homeless people sleeping in cars, getting citations, and being forced to live in shelters, so I had gotten off easy.

Once I recline my seat, kick off my shoes, and wrap myself in a blanket, I remind Shannon why we're in this situation. There's not a night I don't rehearse the same story; she'll never forget that her father has us in this predicament. Shannon kicks me again, not wanting to hear the story. But I know she'll be on my side if I add more details this time. I need her support. My family is back East, and we've never been close, so I can't count on them. My mother is the only relative in California, but she lives in a shelter. One would think after years of poverty, she would've broken the cycle. She passed down this bad luck to me, and here I sit.

Dex was a good boyfriend at first. There weren't any red flags I missed. It's odd how people can present one way and then change when a child is in the picture. This humbling realization about Dex makes me empathize with my mother. Chances are she didn't miss any signs when it came to the many men she entertained. Most men are cheaters and deceitful, so they likely sold her some story to get her panties off, and she fell for the lies. What woman doesn't want to hear a man say he'd be faithful and love her and only her?

If I weren't afraid of my mother laughing at my situation, I'd contact her. But I've been critical of her over the years. I doubt she'd have an encouraging word for me. As an only child, I have no siblings to lean on. I don't make friends easily with women since, in the past, they've gone after my boyfriends, so there are no friends other than this nice lady Barbara I met since becoming homeless. She lives in her car, too, and parks a few blocks away from me. I run into her when I use the restroom at the park.

My thoughts come back to Dex and how he betrayed me. We met last year when I started a new job at a recycling company. Dex is the manager, and we often found ourselves stealing glances or me touching his arm while laughing at his jokes. We exchanged numbers not long after and began dating. The relationship was a secret since we didn't want coworkers in our business. Within two months, I moved in with him.

Shannon is moving again. Something tells me she's judging me. It saddens me that Shannon will grow up resenting me like I did my mother. More determined to gain her acceptance, I continue telling Shannon my story, although she doesn't want to hear it. Nothing my mother ever said helped me comprehend why we were homeless. Or why, when we got an apartment, we kept getting evicted. In my eyes, she was a failure. The cycle is repeating between Shannon and me, but I don't know how to end it.

Dex and I were good until we weren't. We were going to build together. I met his family, and they liked me. I couldn't have wished for a better man. We talked about marriage and having kids down the line. A manager position opened at work, and he encouraged me to apply, but before I could, I got pregnant. I'll never forget the day I told him I was pregnant.

"Why did you have to go and mess up a good thing, Hannah? You said you were on the pill." Dex had never raised his voice at me or looked at me like I was an idiot. To say the least, I didn't appreciate how he handled the news. We should've been celebrating.

"I am on the pill. You act like I tried to trap you. You said we'd have a family someday. Well, that day came sooner than expected."

"You can't be responsible with your birth control, so it makes me doubt you in other areas. I can't trust you. Get rid of the baby, and we'll try again in the future." I slapped him. I should've kept my hands to myself, but I was angry. Why would he want to get rid of our child?

Here Shannon goes, judging me again. She interrupts every time I tell her the story of me and Dex. I sense her saying I'm a bad mother for saying how her father responded. It was inappropriate, but I need her to know I'm the one who was here for her, not her father. Had I listened to him, I wouldn't be six months pregnant. I deserve a pat on the back for keeping Shannon.

Not long after refusing to have the abortion, I got suspicious of Dex and began following him. He started buying new underwear and cologne and stayed out later. Had I not followed him, I wouldn't be homeless now. I'm making assumptions. He would've thrown me out sooner or later, but I took my destiny into my own hands and left him. Sad thing is, he didn't try to stop me.

One evening, I followed him to the grocery store and waited in my car for him to come out. I felt like a fool. After all, he was at the store, probably getting something to cook for us. It was his night to cook. The new underwear and cologne must've been to please me. He had been giving me the silent treatment, so I had assumed he was seeing someone else. Or he saw the error in his way and was preparing to repair things between us. Instead of going home, I stayed in the car, checking social media. Dex exited the store with a flower arrangement, convincing me he still loved me. In his other hand, he carried a bag of groceries. I had nothing to worry about.

When he pulled off, I followed a few cars behind. Had he spotted me, I would have said it was a coincidence we were near one another. Once he turned in a direction not toward our home, I told myself he needed to get gas or stop at another store. But he made a left into a residential area. To remain inconspicuous, I parked a few cars away. I knew everyone he knew; not one person stayed in that area. I wondered what he was up to when he got out of the car with my flowers and groceries and walked to a house where a woman, who looked nothing like me opened the door. They kissed and then went inside. What had he seen in her? She wore long braids and was muscular, like a female bodybuilder. I was thin and of average height, and she was much taller. I had no plans to fight her since I was pregnant. Truthfully, had I not been pregnant, I wouldn't have started anything with her.

Devastated that Dex would cheat on me, especially while I carried his child, I got out of the car and headed to the woman's house to confront him. As much time as we spent together before the pregnancy, his new relationship must've begun when I told him about Shannon. He moved fast, and that hurt. He had already begun buying the new woman flowers and groceries and surprising her at her house. I shouldn't have been surprised, seeing how quickly things had progressed between us. I wasn't ready to give Dex up since I had allowed myself to be put in a desperate situation.

Before moving in with Dex, I rented a room from an old married couple. Since leaving them, they got a new tenant. I doubted I could afford a studio since it had taken me forever to find that room for such a low price. Los Angeles isn't cheap, and I didn't have enough money saved to leave Dex without ending up in a homeless shelter. I also had to prove my mother wrong to show I was better than her. So, a lot was riding on my ability to make things work for Dex and me. Like it or not, he was a father, and my baby and I needed him.

Like the classy lady I was, I knocked and then beat on the door when they took too long answering. To my surprise, Dex answered the door too comfortably for my liking. That fast, he had slipped into a robe and slippers. He stepped outside. "How did you get this address? Are you following me? What do you want?"

He had lost his mind, treating me as if something was wrong with me. He wouldn't let me get a word in, asking back-to-back questions. Once he paused, I went in. "Why are you here instead of at home with me? Did you tell your woman I'm pregnant with your child?" I pushed Dex and screamed into the house. I was losing him and wanted that chick to know she was helping destroy a happy home.

Surprisingly, Dex pushed me, ensuring I didn't enter the house. Why did he put his hands on me? After years of homelessness, I learned how to protect myself. So, I spit on him. Before I knew it, the muscular chick came out of the house, and they both tackled me to the ground, where they restrained me until a neighbor got them off me. I could understand the woman attacking me because she didn't know me and likely didn't know I was pregnant. But Dex's behavior was inexcusable. Not only did he hate me, but he also hated our child because I could've miscarried.

While on the ground, I cursed and hollered, but they wouldn't let me up until the neighbors intervened. Although in pain, I limped to my car when I heard sirens. The last thing I needed was to go to jail while pregnant. My life with Dex was over. He made his decision, and unfortunately, it wasn't to be with me and his child.

I sped to the house, packed what I could, and left. Seeing as Dex put hands on me, nothing would stop him from sending the police to our house.

That was months ago, the last day I saw him. I never returned to work to avoid Dex.

Inside my car, I have yet to fall asleep. It's like this every night, me thinking about Dex. He and his woman haven't heard the last of me. Why should he live well while Shannon and I are homeless? My nightly routine involves texting him, the only form of communication we have, asking him to send money for Shannon and me, and I'll think about not putting him on child support. Each time he types the same response. At this point, I think it's copied and pasted. *It's not my baby. Move on with your life.*

Why must I torture myself, hoping he'll respond differently? Dex is over me and our child. I'm always in a terrible mood and feel worse after he responds. No one will mediate for me and Dex. After things went bad, I reached out to his family and friends, but they never responded and blocked me. I expected more from them even though they were his people. They know Shannon and I are homeless, yet they haven't offered a care package or a blanket. People suck, and so does my life. I have no job and nothing to do so each day passes slowly. My mornings and afternoons consist of collecting recyclables and cashing them in, but certainly not at the recycling center where I once worked. Sometimes, people at the park offer me money out of pity. My back seat has some of my belongings, and my trunk is filled with my belongings, a sign of homelessness. I wish people weren't in my business, but it's hard not to show I'm struggling. The only people I talk to regularly are Barbara and the workers at the recycling center. Shannon has had enough of my story, and I'm tired of talking. I get comfortable in my car seat and drift off to sleep.

The next day, after recycling, I sit on a park bench, eating a sandwich and chips when Barbara joins me. "Hannah, what are you up to today?" she asks in that cheery voice I find so annoying. It baffles me how she can be positive and broke. I wonder why she asks me the same thing daily when she knows I don't have a job.

"Nothing much. Just eating and enjoying time with Shannon."

To my shock, she rubs my belly. We're cool, but not that cool. I hold back my disapproval to avoid alienating myself further. "You're six months, but don't look pregnant at all. Have you seen a doctor? You should be showing by now."

"The doctor says stress is causing the baby to be smaller. But I can't help how I feel these days. I talk to Shannon every day to let her know we'll be all right." I lie about the doctor because I don't need Barbara too much in my business. It's bad enough that she knows I'm homeless. I can't have her assuming I'm a bad mother by not going to the doctor. Life has been too chaotic to visit a clinic. I eat as healthy as I can to ensure Shannon develops well.

"Life is too good to spend it stressed, thinking about the past. I stay in my car because it's just me, but if I had a kid, I'd go to a shelter. Have you given a shelter more thought? It gets cold in the car in the winter."

This is why I don't open up to people much. They all assume they know better than the next person. I'm not stupid. If she knows so much, why is she homeless? "I plan to get out of this situation before winter," I lie again. I tell Barbara how much I hate Dex and his woman. Despite her eye-rolling, I continue the story, needing someone other than Shannon to talk to.

Barbara stands to leave. "I'm not trying to be insensitive, but you must let that man go. He didn't choose you, baby. Put him on child support, move into a shelter to get help with housing, and go on about your life. You're still young."

Before I can respond, she waves me off and walks down the hill. What sense is it having friends if they can't accept me at my lowest? Who did she think she was talking to? Excuse me for not being cheery and having stories of enlightenment to share. One thing she said that stays with me is that winter is approaching. I dread myself or Shannon being uncomfortable. The heat wave that passed weeks ago was horrific, and I survived, yet I couldn't imagine sleeping in the car during winter. Dex got me into the situation, and it's up to him to get me out of it.

NOT LONG AFTER, I'm at the apartment I once shared with Dex, and someone else lives there and has no knowledge of Dex. I ask the woman if Dex left a forwarding address, but she becomes irritable and closes the door in my face. It's as if the life I had with him never existed. Was I that easy to get over? There's nothing about me he wanted to fight for. He never loved me if he could move on so quickly, although I made his life comfortable. My every waking day was to please him. I even bought dumb relationship books he suggested we read together. Why did he have me learn about love languages if he wasn't going to love me?

Desperate, I end up at the job where I used to work with Dex, and my coworkers aren't glad to see me. Dex poisoned them against me. Instead of hugging and congratulating me on being further along in my pregnancy, they accuse me of stalking Dex and say to leave or they'll call the police. I comply.

Stalking? I've never been accused of that. Dex ruined my reputation among everyone we know. Although I despise him, I still love him. It must be my hormones talking. I threatened him with child support, but I wouldn't go through with it if he took me back and got rid of his quarterback girlfriend, assuming they're still together. I'm twenty-seven and scared to be a single mother. I deserve a stable life, and so does Shannon. Once I get back with Dex, if he continues to cheat, after I have Shannon, I'll make Dex pay for a babysitter so I can find a new job and save money. Just when he thinks it's good between us, I'll leave and then put him on child support. I won't share my thoughts on this with Barbara, who'll say I'm dumb. Her opinion doesn't matter. I have Shannon to think of. Dex will think he's getting over on me, but I'll win in the end. I'm not confident he'll want to build a family together, but I'll never know if I don't ask. Love can't be erased easily.

Soon after, I park at Dex's mother's house. She hasn't seen me since I announced my pregnancy. Once she hears me out, her heart will soften toward Shannon and me, and she'll talk to Dex. He's grown, but his mother's words weigh heavy on him. It bothers me that his mother didn't come to my defense before. She's always been a kind woman, full of wisdom. Her ignoring my texts means she has an unhealthy relationship with Dex I didn't notice before. She must assume that if he marries me and we start a family, she'll lose her son. Her husband died years ago, and Dex is an only child. The old woman is lonely. I'll make her see I'm not trying to take her son from her.

I knock at her door and put on my fakest smile when she opens the door to let her know I come in peace. She peeks her head out the door like she's scared of me, yet I'm no stranger. I get to the point. "Can you talk some sense into Dex? He's ignoring me, and it ain't right. I want to talk to him so he can be a part of Shannon's life." To avoid looking desperate, I won't mention I want to rekindle a relationship with Dex.

She says through the cracked door, "How do you know where I live? I called the police and told Dex to have the police waiting for you at his place in case you show up there. You need help. You attacked my son, and the police have been looking for you. Stop stalking us."

She's delusional, calling me a stalker and pretending like I've never been to her house. Dex and I didn't visit regularly, but I wouldn't forget her address. Mothers should love their children, but not to the point of upholding them when wrong. This is a problem with society: not enough parents correcting their young and adult children. I never want to be the kind of mother who doesn't tell my child right from wrong. "I was upset that day. I didn't try to hurt him—"

She cut me off, "—You a lie. I was there, looking out the window. Who do you think called the police? You lucky I didn't come out there and put my foot up your ass."

Now I see where Dex gets his dysfunctional ways. She was aware he was cheating, and she said nothing. Perhaps I can understand her not getting into his business. However, why would she be at the new chick's house? That's just messy. Since his mother condones cheating, I don't think I want her in Shannon's life. She stood by watching Dex and his bodybuilder tackle me, knowing I was pregnant. In my mind, that means she wants Shannon dead. Once Dex and I are back together, I can't put my foot down and say his mother can't see Shannon. But I'll keep an eye on his mother.

"I see you won't be of any help, Mom." I've never called her mom, but I'm getting my man back, so she had better get used to me. When Dex sees how big my stomach has grown, he'll come running back to me. This'll be the last day I'm homeless. "Me and Shannon are leaving."

As I walk to my car, she yells, "Who is Shannon?"

I ignore her; slow people are annoying. She insinuated I'm mental, but she's asking stupid questions. I've never told her the baby's name, but Dex should've told her. I hate to gossip, but his mother might be on drugs. That would explain her acting like a different person and talking to me through the door. She should blame Dex for me spitting on him. Men drive women to their breaking point and then become shocked when they snap. He should be lucky I didn't set that chick's house on fire. And then I'd be the one to blame for the flames. Rest in peace, Left Eye.

"Leave me and Dex alone!" his ghetto mother keeps screaming, but I keep it classy and get in my car.

Before pulling off, I text Dex, letting him know we should be together. He replies that we'll never be a couple and that he wants to let a nice family adopt Shannon because his girlfriend is pregnant. I drop my phone and scream. Shannon kicks uncontrollably. He doesn't want a child with me, but he's having one with another woman? What is it about me and Shannon that he hates? Did I not encourage him enough? I tried peace, but men like him only learn to treat women right when forced to. I know just what to do to regain my respect. I'm done begging him to do right by me and Shannon. The woman he's with must be better than me. Maybe her sex is better. Or she cooks better. She has more muscles than him, so I imagine not many men want her. She might be paying Dex to be with her. Many men want to be wined and dined; it wouldn't surprise me if he's allowing that chick to take care of him. Who knows, but I'm done figuring out why he chose her.

After composing myself, I go to the gas station and get supplies. Before leaving, I play my mother's favorite song, "I Wish" by Carl Thomas. I wish I never met Dexter Montgomery; however, I don't regret Shannon.

At Dex's chick's house, I get out of the car with the gas can and lighter. I won't kill them; I only want them to come out of the house to hear me out. My tactic is drastic, yet Dex has driven me to this. On their lawn, I splash gasoline on the grass, and before I can light a match, someone screams, "Put your hands up, Hannah Sheldon! We got a call you'd be on your way here." It's the police.

Confused, I look around, and there are no police cars. Dex's mother is a snitch. Other officers jump out of unmarked cars and rush me with their guns trained on me. When they have the lighter and gas can out of my hands, they read me my rights. My mind is racing, trying to comprehend what happens next. Will I spend time in jail or prison?

Can I convince them I was only going to burn the grass? Most importantly, will they take Shannon from me? Shannon will hate me. I can't escape this cycle of bad mothering and poverty. The police are asking questions. I tune them out to avoid further incriminating myself.

Dex and his girlfriend run to me with fingers pointed in my face. Something is different about Dex's girlfriend. She has blue and black braids down her back, but she now has a mustache with a high-pitched voice. The last time I saw her, she was muscular but didn't look like a man. I must be overwhelmed and not seeing things clearly. The woman must have polycystic ovary syndrome and forgot to shave this morning. Two officers step between Dex and me and Dex's girlfriend.

Dex screams at me, "Are you for real? What's wrong with you? I'm gay. I've never been in a relationship with you. Stop stalking me." He turns to the officers. "Get her out of here and lock her up. I don't know why it's taken this long to find her."

Now he's gay. How can he be when I'm pregnant, and he told me his girlfriend is too? He never ceases to amaze me with the lies he creates. He'll say anything to get me locked up, despite me carrying his seed. This is funny. I stay quiet to hear what other lies Dex will tell.

The officer says to Dex, "There's been a warrant for her arrest, but this is the first time we've seen her. She violated the stay-away order. She'll finally get some help."

Dex got an order against me after he played with my heart and manipulated me. He's playing the victim role well.

Dex's chick tells the officer, "Like we told you, Hannah worked with Dex and began stalking him when he fired her for obsessing over him. We're gay men."

I'm laughing uncontrollably. Gay men. His woman must identify as a man. Though she's built like a bodybuilder, she was born a woman. Why would Dex want a transgender? Now I get it. He left me because he's now living in his truth. At least I know nothing is wrong with me. I would've never suspected Dexter is gay. There were no signs. He could've told me the truth about his sexual orientation. I've heard enough. I wish the police would uncuff me so I can leave. If they're going to take me to jail, then they should hurry. Anything is better than being here with Dex.

"She keeps texting, talking about she's pregnant." Dex points at my stomach. "Her belly is the same size as when she worked at the recycling center. I was kind to her, and this is how she reacts. Everyone at work, including Hannah, knows I'm gay. She needs help."

Suddenly, I get a flashback of how I met Dex and my time at the recycling center. It's so clear I can't deny it. Dex isn't lying, after all. What's wrong with me? He is gay, and so is his partner, Diamond, who used to come eat lunch with him all the time. How could I forget? Diamond always wore bright-colored braids.

Why would my mind convince me of things that didn't happen? Something must've transpired between me and Dex. I wouldn't make all of this up. I got pregnant somehow. "Dex," I say. "You must've cheated with me." But why would I have sex with a gay man? "This is your baby girl I'm pregnant with. Shannon is real."

"I don't know if she's real or not!" yells Dex. "Go find your real baby daddy. Stalking me and my momma is crazy. I've never had sex with a woman and never will." As if his words didn't hurt enough, he says, "And you don't look pregnant." He and Diamond hug as if they've gone through hell. To crush me further, he says, "See, I'm gay, gay, gay, real gay."

Diamond and Dex follow the officer to the porch, and I can no longer hear them. Diamond keeps shooting me evil looks, and I can't blame her for being angry. Apparently, my mind made up some things that weren't real, but I'm wondering how I got pregnant. Dex is wrong about one thing: I'm pregnant. Maybe he and I met for happy hour one day, got drunk, and had sex. My head hurts, and I give up my search for answers. I trust I'll get another flashback that fills in more pieces. Why am I having memory loss? Is something wrong with me?

As an officer puts me in a cop car, I warn him to be careful about the baby. After he gets into the car, he says, "You escaped from Hamilton Psychiatric Facility months ago, and we must return you because you're a danger to yourself and others." The officer is out of his mind, and I can't believe my tax dollars pay for his job. He tells me I've been in and out of Hamilton Psychiatric Facility since age eighteen after my mother got stabbed to death at a homeless shelter. My mother is alive and living in a shelter. If he takes these cuffs off me, I could call her. "I'm sorry you've had it so bad, Hannah."

Attempting to tune him out, I rub my stomach to soothe Shannon. She doesn't like what the officer is saying, and neither do I. Dex turned him against me, and now he's in on the lie. I wonder how much Dex is paying him to torment Shannon and me. The officer continues. "Thanks to you, the recycling center got busted for paying under the table. Had they gone about things the right way, we would've caught you long ago once your name and social security number entered the system."

When we drive away, I say, "Take me to the hospital so I can check on my baby. If you're taking me to jail afterward, fine. But I'm not going to a nutty institution because I've never been mental."

The officer driving says, "You're not pregnant. The folks at Hamilton say you've been saying that you're pregnant since they met you."

No matter what the cop says, Shannon is real, and our bond will continue to grow. Everyone is lying. Even the flashback I had about meeting Dex with his partner, Diamond, isn't real. I must've gotten confused hearing Dex and his muscular girlfriend lie. Boy, they're good. They had me believing them. Per usual, I tell Shannon about her scheming father, and she kicks.

Dex and I fell in love after meeting at the recycling center. I moved in with him shortly after, and he changed on me when he found out I was pregnant. When the officers remind me that I'm not pregnant, I'm aware I'm talking to Shannon aloud. Never one to get distracted from telling a good story, I continue not caring if they hear me. After all, Shannon will grow up knowing why I'm a single mother and why her father isn't around: Dex is a lying manipulator who abandoned me and made me homeless after learning I was pregnant with his baby girl—Shannon.

The End

the motivational speaker

. . .

IT'S hard to fathom that I, Leighton Lorenzo, am standing in the rain, waiting to get inside the building to see a motivational speaker. Self-improvement has always been Guyton's thing, never mine. I'm secure in the woman I am and don't require someone to pump me up to feel good about myself. Had I done more things Guyton liked when we were together, we might still be married. I'm here today to learn all I need to know about Mr. Harold Graham, the motivational speaker who convinced Guyton to leave me. When I'm done with him, his career will be over, and he'll die a disgraced man.

The line moves, and everyone cheers. People behind me are doting on the man of the hour. It disgusts me that humans seek a savior rather than looking within where all answers lie. I'm not easily impressed, so he'll have to do or say something amazing for me to believe his tickets are worth three hundred dollars. I stare at the silly people in front and behind me, wondering how they could be so gullible to pay this kind of money for advice one could find free online.

Once we take our seats, I expect to see Mr. Harold Graham. Instead, comedians are the opening act. They are decent, but they're not Dave Chappelle or Katt Williams. I wasn't expecting comedy at this type of event, yet I feel less cheated for the money I paid to be here. I imagine I would've laughed harder if my feet were dry. My umbrella is on its last leg, so some parts of me got wet. The host introduces the man of the hour. Everyone is clapping as if the president graced us with his presence. To fit in, I stand. I'm in the front row and must play the part.

Harold Graham is dressed in a suit that fits him well. Although he's on the stage, I notice his shoes shining from where I'm seated, and his watch is glistening. He might not have any words of wisdom to add to my life, but at least he looks the part. The man is smart. He knows you must dress well to get attention. If people think he's rich, the masses will believe anything he says and buy whatever he's selling. He has loads of tables in the lobby with his books and other merchandise. I could take some pointers from this con artist. He's making eye contact with all of us in the front seats while showing off his award-winning smile. The man knows what it takes to bring in the big bucks. If he hadn't ruined my marriage, I might date him. He's hustling, but if people are dumb enough to be taken, why not abuse them?

To my dismay, Harold Graham makes us greet our neighbors and tell them one thing we hope to get from today's lecture. I hesitantly introduce myself with a fake name to a woman named Sherita. My intentions here aren't pure; no need to tell anyone my identity. Glancing at her shoes, I no longer care what she says. Sherita is wearing flat shoes she must've gotten from Target. I shouldn't judge her since she's probably here to learn to level up. Don't get me started on her wig that's not properly glued to her scalp. I want to hug the poor woman who is here to learn to be her best possible self. Instead, I say I hope she gets all she wants and more. What does being her best self even mean? If she won't give more definite answers, she should sit.

I lie to Sherita, saying I hope to learn how to present myself more professionally to get new customers and increase customer satisfaction. When she asks what business I'm in, I'm taken aback. I hadn't planned on that. She seems satisfied when I say I sell haircare supplies. Sharita is embarrassed when I stare at her wig. Someone should've told her it's time to throw it in the trash. The women she came with aren't her friends. If she learns anything from this conference, it should be to surround herself with better people. Now she's whispering to her friends, I suppose, about me, yet I'm unbothered. I'm always authentic and say what comes to mind. If I cared more, I'd call Sherita out for talking about me. Life has been unkind to her based on her looks, so I won't cause problems for her.

Harold Graham shouts something and is now asking us to repeat it. Had I been paying attention, I could participate. Being here in front of my ex-husband's guru, I can't keep my mind off Guyton. I wonder how he'd feel if he knew I was here. I'm surprised he's not here on opening night. He wouldn't miss this event and will certainly attend another night. Although the speaker lives in our city, he has more out-of-town speaking engagements than in town.

The night Guyton told me he was filing for divorce is still troubling. He went from loving and worshiping me one day to ending things the next.

"Leighton, I'm leaving you," Guyton said, after asking me to join him at our spacious dining room table. His coldness was new. He didn't allow me to protest, nor did he ask if I was okay with his decision. All I could do was collect my thoughts while staring at the table. Of all the things to think about, I wondered, had I let him invite friends over for dinner, would it have stopped him from asking for a divorce? We had bought a large dining set even though it was just us two because Guyton aspired to entertain guests. However, I always found a reason not to entertain, and he went along with it. My home was my sanctuary, and I was raised to believe friends remain friends if you keep them out of your house.

"You don't mean this. What's up with you? You wouldn't be able to survive without me." Looking back, I should've taken a gentler approach. No man wants to hear those words, even if they're true. I wanted him to stay, but I was too hurt to be vulnerable. I'm not the begging type.

"I figured you say that. You never cease to amaze me. I'm leaving tonight and will be back for my things."

The smug expression he had was evident my power over him had decreased. He had forgotten I was the boss in the relationship. I had to remind him who was running things. If a woman didn't show a man who was in charge, he'd run over her. My mother taught me that. "Whatever you leave with today is all you'll be taking out of this house. If you pack and go, don't come back. I suggest you think long and hard before you destroy the life we built."

"If I must get the courts involved, I will. Both our names are on this house. We paid equally for everything. My name ain't Tina Turner. Don't expect me to leave empty-handed."

At the time, I found it funny he mentioned Tina Turner. Guyton had taken my last name since I refused to take his. My last name is Lorenzo, and his name is Roach. Leighton Roach—I think not. I wouldn't have taken it even if he had a proper last name. I had to be in control. His parents took issue with me not taking his last name and told him I'd never respect him. They were right. But it was more to it than him accepting my last name. He wasn't dominant.

When we met, we both were available, and I was getting older, so I selected him. He was handsome, made good money, and we both liked the finer things in life. Though he wanted kids, when I wouldn't bend, he backed off. I had him wrapped around my finger until he asked for a divorce.

"Who put you up to this? You're not smart enough to think of something like this on your own. If you leave me, who'll do the thinking for you?"

He had always been easy to control, so when he said he was leaving, I knew someone had gotten into his head. Guyton was forever second-guessing himself and required constant validation. For years, his parents had been in his ear to leave me, but he never listened. So, it could not have been them who planted a rebellious seed. Neither had he made new friends whom I could blame. The ones he did have were used to him bowing to me and had long given up on trying to make him man up.

"Does it matter?" asked Guyton. "You don't love me."

I could've defended myself all that night. "The only reason you have your current position at work is because I was your cheerleader. Is this what you want?" I needed my man to stay. My single friends had it hard in the dating world, and I didn't want to join them. I wasn't a young woman; my options would be slimmer than they were in my twenties and thirties. I figured Guyton found a younger, submissive woman. Just like a man in his forties to push aside the wife who built with him to find a younger woman who knew nothing of the struggle. She'd look at him like her hero, while I saw him for what he was: nothing without me.

Guyton hadn't drunk wine in years but left the dining room table and poured us wine. Looking back, he might have needed the courage to leave me. Saying it and doing it were two different things. He had been full of surprises that night. I accepted the wine and gulped it down to calm my nerves.

Out of nowhere, he said, "Harold Graham says a man must take bold actions in every area of his life. Timidity is for the weak. No one respects a passive man."

"Who the hell is Harold Graham?" I asked. "And why have you involved him in our business?"

"He's a motivational speaker. I sent you a few of his videos, and I'm guessing you didn't watch them. You're never interested in the things I'm into, another reason I'm leaving you. And I'm tired of you talking down to me. Harold Graham says everyone deserves peace in their home. Without it, everything else we do in life will crumble. He says to divorce everything that eats at you like a cankerworm. You're my worm." Guyton continued to spout off more Harold Graham sayings, so I blocked him out. He was lucky I didn't pour the remainder of the wine on his head for calling me a worm. I began listening again after he said, "Heal yourself so you can stop destroying others around you. The only people you surround yourself with are other mean girls." He stood and looked out the dining room floor-length windows as if in deep thought. I was on the verge of interrupting his lengthy pause until he said with his back turned to me, "I'm done."

Guyton packed his things that night, and I watched him from our king-sized bed without interruption. His words had stung. No one had ever called me nice, but mean was a stretch. I was the most evolved and healed person I knew. While Guyton readied himself to leave me, I called my girls, and they reminded me how awesome I was with or without Guyton. He mumbled to himself and slammed things since I talked to my friends while in the same room with him. My girls reminded me how great I was. I was a fashion designer for some important people in the city. My hair, nails, and clothes always looked good. For an older woman, I turned heads. Not as many as I once did, but I didn't do bad. Who was I without Guyton? Another unmarried black woman. How pathetic. I didn't want that for my black sisters, let alone myself.

I had assumed Guyton needed time to cool off. He'd be back, so I thought. When I got off the phone with my friends, I researched Harold Graham, desperate to know who he was and what gave him the right to empower Guyton. I was all the strength Guyton needed.

After Guyton moved out, he never texted or called. Our only communication was with him serving me divorce papers, which I signed. There was nothing left to fight for. I could've called or texted him, but it would've made me look desperate. He was the one who left me, so he should've contacted me.

At the divorce proceeding, we split everything and sold the house and furniture. We had a clean break; no kids involved. Recently, a mutual friend told me Guyton's parents were happy he was free of me. I never liked his folks.

Guyton wasn't dating anyone and was still single. I had assumed that a year and a half later, he would've moved on. No man stayed with me long term until Guyton, who stuck it out nine years. If not for Harold Graham, we'd still be together.

After Guyton's treachery, my business suffered. He was never a gossip when we were together, but the moment he left me, he couldn't keep my name out of his mouth. He repeated many of our private conversations and had the audacity to tell people I belittled him. It was true. Guyton made good money, and I never wanted him to think he was better than me. It was my way of keeping him in his place. How could it be my fault if he believed the nasty things I said? His self-esteem was low, so he should've blamed his parents. A stronger man would've let what I said come in one ear and out the other. Whatever I did to him should've stayed between us. He slandered me to so many people it got back to my clients, resulting in clients canceling and ignoring me when I reached out to them. I don't blame Guyton. I blame Harold Graham.

Bringing myself back to the present, I'm bored. Harold Graham is failing to enlighten me. Everyone is shouting, jumping out of their seats, and taking notes. The man is repeating quotes I see online. "Keep your circle tight," says Harold Graham. "Stop letting everyone know your next move because they aren't in your corner like you think. Many are plotting your downfall."

Guyton was naïve, but to buy into Harold Graham's teachings means he's slower than suspected. When Harold Graham forces us to leave our comfort zones, the rest of the audience and I introduce ourselves to ten people and tell them what we do for a living. Everyone exchanges business cards except for me. I'm here to spy on Harold Graham, not network. I wonder if I could get a refund after this event.

A handsome man introduces himself, asks me out, and gives me his information. I still got it. I'll never call him because he appears too confident. I don't have time for alpha male energy, so I give him a fake name and say I'll be in touch.

Finally, the meeting has ended, and now I can go into action. Many people, including myself, meet Harold Graham at the front of the room to shake his hand. When it's my turn to talk one on one, I put on my best flirting act, and am not sure he's into me. He gives the same smile to everyone, but then he grabs my hand, holds it a while, and asks me questions about myself. The questions are like the ones he asked others about their personal and career goals, but the bedroom eyes he's giving me tell me he's into me. Harold and I disregard the people hissing and rolling their eyes because I'm taking too much time. I can't stop staring at his teeth, wondering how much he paid for them. In an older picture of him online, he had a crooked smile. Before I become his worst nightmare, I'll have to ask who his dentist is.

"I'd love to network with you after this meeting. The things you said about keeping one's circle tight really moved me," I lie, and he's grinning like he believes me. "If I could talk to you more about a few things, I'm certain I could live my best life. I have a habit of giving too much, especially to men. I need your help." His eyes fall to my cleavage, and he quickly catches himself. This dress hugs every curve and props up my boobs, so I can't blame him for looking.

"I'd like to connect with you more, Leighton." I've told him my name once, and he already remembers it, which is why they pay him the big bucks, I'm assuming, because his message isn't worth a penny. "Wait for me, and we can get coffee to discuss your needs." He wants me. Mission accomplished.

After he finishes talking to his sheep, he asks if I'd like to go get something to eat so we can discuss his mentoring me. But first, he must stop by his house to change into something more comfortable. He's not fooling me. He thinks he'll get me into his home and seduce me. When he gives me his address, I agree to meet him there.

NOT LONG AFTER, I pull up to Harold's huge house in a neighborhood where people probably never see their neighbors because the houses are far apart. It must be nice to have this kind of money. He meets me at my car and says, "I'll be back, beautiful. Don't go anywhere." When he winks, I almost forget to wink back. It's been a while since I've flirted. Although I dominated Guyton, I never cheated or entertained men. One would think Guyton would've given me bonus points for my faithfulness, but some men don't appreciate a good woman.

"How about I come in and make you something to eat? Or we can order in." He must agree to this. How else will I get inside his house to destroy his life? I ensured I looked my best so I'd be chosen. No way will he pass up sex.

"I wish I could, but the maids don't come until tomorrow. Maybe next time."

"Don't worry about a mess. I won't judge you." I open my door, but he blocks it.

"Not tonight. Give me a few minutes." He walks away and goes indoors.

This isn't how I imagined things going. If I'm going to accuse him of raping me, I need to get inside his house. I could remain in the car and try to get him to a hotel after dinner, but patience isn't my virtue. Once people think Harold Graham is a rapist, they'll cancel him, and he'll have a lot of court fees. I'm prepared to be on the news and blogs telling my horrific night of surviving Harold Graham. My business will pick up because people will feel sorry for me, and Guyton will come running into my arms, distraught that his icon raped me. My dear Guyton will have no choice but to nurse me back to health.

When I get out of the car, I knock at the front door and wait. There's no answer after a few minutes. I try to peek inside a window but can't see anything. Why is it so dark inside? He likely hates light since he always has bright lights shining on him. I knock again, but still no answer. Something tells me to turn the doorknob, and I follow my intuition, letting myself into his house.

Once I step into the foyer, theatrical smoke, the kind used at night-clubs, hits me in the face. Over the loud, slow jams, I call Harold's name and get no answer. When he shows his face, I'll tell him I have to use the bathroom. I tried knocking, but he didn't answer. After turning the corner into a large open space, the only lights are blue and red strobe lights, and naked women with dog chains around their necks dance in five cages along the walls. It looks like a strip club and nothing like a residence. Two couches are the only furniture in the center of the room. He must use the place for himself and other men needing an escape from their wives. Harold Graham doesn't notice me; he's standing outside a cage caressing a woman. No wonder he left me in the car. The women see me but say nothing and keep dancing. Harold has his own private strip show. I'm out of here, but before I go, let me get this on video. The footage will be better than lying about him raping me. I hate that the women in the cages would allow him to degrade them, but it's not my business. They look happy to be here, and I suspect he pays well.

When I pull out my phone and look up, a burly man is heading toward me, and he doesn't appear happy to see me. I prepare to lie to him about why I'm in the house now that he's in my face. He raises his hand before I get the chance, and I black out.

Some time later, I awake on the couch with Harold Graham staring down at me. "Leighton, didn't I tell you to stay in the car? You should've listened. I'm always forgetting to lock my door because it's a safe neighborhood."

Although my head is throbbing, I attempt to stand, but the burly guy pushes me down. Harold Graham says, "You know you can't leave now. I can't have you telling people what you've seen. And to think, I had every intention of dating you and letting you live free." He points at the cages. "Welcome to Graham's Playground."

"I haven't seen a thing. I needed to use the bathroom. Let me go, and we can forget about this."

Harold Graham and the big guy look at one another in disbelief. He says to the fat man, "They all say the same thing. Silly woman thinks we're dumb." He turns to me. "You might as well get comfortable since you aren't leaving. You'll like it here; they all do. I and the girls will teach you everything you need to know about your place as a woman and how to serve men."

He didn't know me at all; he'd better recruit someone else. I must get out of this. "I want to go home. People will be looking for me. Why are you doing this?"

"Shh," Harold says. "Get naked. I've been dying to see what you look like underneath that dress."

When he licks his lips, I'm disgusted. They could kill me, and my parents would never see me again. Are they sex traffickers? Why would they want me, a forty-six-year-old woman? The big guy is looking at me like he wants to rip my clothes off. I stand, but Harold Graham slaps the hell out of me.

"You'll learn to obey me. I haven't given you permission to get up. I'll tell you one last time. Strip. And refer to me as sir when answering me," Harold says in a menacing tone, ensuring I get the message.

When I refuse, the big guy holds me down while Harold Graham takes off my clothes. Once the big one slings me over his shoulder, they place me in a cage with a woman who acts like this is another day for her. These women, too, must be here against their will. Observing the other women, I see they all have nice bodies and are pros. Nothing about me screams exotic dancer, but maybe if I comply, I can go home. Harold Graham and the man sit on the couch and tell me to dance or else. What does 'or else' mean?

The woman near me puts her back to the bars while she dances. I assume she doesn't want our captors to hear us. Over the music, she says, "Move your body, or they'll kill you. The fat one beat a woman to death. Stop crying because you'll never get out of here. They kidnapped me, and I don't know how long I've been here. Do yourself a favor and obey. They feed us good, and we have our own rooms. I'm Candy, by the way."

"I'm Leighton," is all I say. Her words bring no comfort and don't dry my tears. How am I supposed to pull myself together, not knowing my fate? I'd never accept this lifestyle. Somehow, I'll find my way home, and Harold Graham will go to prison. When I plotted to accuse him of rape, I never thought he'd get the best of me. I'm the victim. He ruined my marriage and put a large dent in my income. Because I lack clients, I must do gig work to supplement my income.

Harold Graham enters the cage and points at me. "Dance. You'll be surprised how good you'll get in time." After I turn my back to him, he slaps and kicks me when I'm on the floor. "I said, dance. And act like you want to be here. All the hoes like it here."

Standing, I sway my hips and copy Candy's moves. Harold seems pleased. Removing dollars from his pocket, he throws them at me and Candy. After exiting the cage, he and the big guy sit on the couch and watch me and the others.

The burly one instructs me to dance with Candy, who comes to me, wraps her hands around my waist, and whispers, "Act like you're turned on. They're kinder when we pretend."

Hesitantly, I move sensuously while Candy wiggles her behind against me. We're both naked, and I'm not into women. However, I endure it and allow her to guide me. She's been here longer, and I need an ally.

After Harold Graham tires of watching me perform, he removes me from the cage and places a collar around my neck. With the leash in his hand, he leads me on my knees around through his massive kitchen and dining room. When I stop crawling, he grabs me by my hair, forcing me to comply. No one has ever disrespected me in this way. If shaming me like a dog isn't bad enough, he takes me to the couch, where he and the burly man take turns raping me. Since I won't stop screaming, Harold Graham covers my mouth. The least they could do was ask the women to face the wall. Yet that wouldn't matter because the women aren't making eye contact, and they're continuing to dance as if I'm not being violated.

Who does Harold Graham think he is? He could've used a condom. I might have an incurable disease following this. My guess is these two men have done this to many women. Harold Graham has America fooled, and if I make it out of here, I'll ensure everyone knows about this monster. I zone out while the big one is on top of me, wishing I had treated Guyton better. He had been good to me. The big one slings me over his shoulder and takes me upstairs, where he bathes me and then forces me back downstairs into a cage where I'm made to dance despite my pain.

From outside the cage, Harold says to me, "I'm happy to have met you," blowing me a kiss. "Some of the other girls I'm selling, but not you." He gives me that same big smile he wore back at his event. I found it endearing before, but now it's scary as hell. "I love you. Say it back."

Not wanting him to hit me again, I oblige. "I love you."

In a harsh tone, he says, "I said to call me sir. Do I have to come in there and teach you a lesson?"

"I love you, too, sir."

"Good girl."

Not long after, Harold Graham and the burly guy train guns on the women while taking two at a time out of the cage and leading them to another part of the house.

Candy fills me in, "We finally get to stop working and go to our rooms for the night. Harold chooses a woman to sleep in his bed every night; his way of rewarding us."

"How is laying in bed with a rapist a prize?" I don't know the woman well, but she doesn't seem angry about any of this.

I assume she reads the confusion on my face. "When you've seen as much as I have here, you learn to keep your head down and not say much. I'm not convinced he doesn't watch and listen to us from another room. Follow my lead, and you'll live. I'm one of his favorites, and he hasn't sold me off. This isn't a good life, but only God knows what's awaiting me if I fall into the hands of someone else."

She might have a point. Keeping my mouth shut could be beneficial, especially until I learn more about the daily routine here. We stop talking when Harold Graham unlocks our cell. He leads us upstairs, where each bedroom door has locks on the outside except for one. The big guy shoves Candy into a room, and Harold Graham pulls me into the unlocked room with the biggest bed I've ever seen. Everything is black and gold and looks immaculate, fit for a king. Except it belongs to a maniac, who has no respect for women. A woman must've hurt him, and now he's taking it out on me. He eyes my body hungrily. "You have the honor of sleeping with me tonight, Leighton. I'll be pleasing you all night long. Thank me in advance for what I plan to do to your body."

Avoiding eye contact, I say, "Thank you."

He backhands me and lifts my chin. "Now, what did I tell you?"

"Thank you, sir." I don't know how much of this abuse I can take. I won't make it if I don't learn the rules fast.

Pulling me into his arms, he caresses my back and then slaps me on the behind. "You're safe with me if you listen. Get in bed." I do as he says while he strips and then sets up a video recorder. He climbs on top of me and enters my body like he owns me. Before long, he forces me on top of him and says, "Whenever I smack your ass, shout, "Harold Graham is the best."

I have no choice but to comply. Why did I ever get involved with Harold Graham?

The End

exposed

. . .

AFTER WAITING for the bishop half an hour past the time he should've started the meeting, he enters the room as if he were on time. No apologies. Just a simple hello, and he convened the meeting. This meeting and all the others would be a waste of time. It's always the same message. If we don't bring in more money, our church will close. The bishop has said the same thing for years, but we're still open by God's grace. Or were we spared by the pay decreases everyone took this year, including the bishop? Since I'm making less, my wife and I have been eating canned food most nights. It's gotten so bad that she's gone back to work, although she hasn't worked in years. The good thing is our kids are grown and independent. We could use their help, but I'm too stubborn to ask for it, so Geraldine returned to work part time. She threatens that if money doesn't increase, she'll begin working full time, which I don't want. It's a bruise to my ego not being able to provide for her fully. When we married, I promised I'd protect and provide. And I've done a pretty good job of it until the churchgoers got stingy with their money.

The bishop turns his attention to me and says, "Pastor Tom, have you considered how we might raise more money for the church? There are no dumb answers. Speak freely."

I forgot he posed the question to us at the last meeting and asked us to have suggestions at the next meeting, which is today. My response is an old one that he shot down before, and I assume he will again. But I have nothing new to offer. "It's simple. We need to charge the members to use the confessional. I sit in the booth for hours six days a week and never receive anything more than a thank you."

"Brother, Catholics don't charge members to use the confessional. People will say we're draining our members of their money. It's never been done before." The bishop stares at me like he's waiting for another recommendation, one he'd like this time.

Undeterred, I persist, "That's just it. We're not Catholic. Who cares what people think? If they want to use the service, they should pay. Counselors and therapists get paid; why shouldn't we? None of us are making decent money, and I'm tired of scraping by. If not for the donors, the doors of this place would've been closed years ago."

"You should be grateful for the money you receive. Remember what our dear Apostle Paul said about learning to be content with much or little," says the bishop. "Trust God."

I want to tell him I couldn't care less about what he or the Apostle Paul had to say concerning my money. My pockets are hurting, and it affects not only me but Geraldine. It's not fair to her. The church members come every week to take while giving crumbs. If we collect two offerings during one service, they complain. When we increased the price for the Tuesday taco plates, they had something to say about that. There's no pleasing them. I hold back what I truly want to say to avoid offending the other brothers. Instead, I stare at the ceiling as if in deep thought until the bishop moves on to someone else.

Eager to please the bishop, Pastor Dowling says, "We should start a building fund. Although we're not building a new church, we're saving this one." The bishop gives an approving nod. This shouldn't surprise me. He likes Pastor Dowling more than me. I respect the bishop, but I assert myself when I have something to say, while Pastor Dowling is a people-pleaser.

The bishop says, "Pastor Dowling, you are a man after my own heart. We'll make the announcement this Sunday. But before we do, inform the deacons so they'll be on board and ready to answer any questions the congregation might have." He turns to me with disappointment evident on his face. "Keep thinking, Pastor Tom. Fast and pray if you must. The Lord will speak, but you must listen."

How dare he? He asks for honest input but only wants to hear what's in line with his vision.

I say, "We aren't doing the people any favors, thinking they can get free what others pay for. Respectfully, at least consider reducing the confessional time. You require us to give each person thirty minutes if needed. Reduce it to fifteen."

Pastor Dowling comes to the rescue as if I disrespected the bishop. "The extra time in the confessional is ensuring our congregation feels supported by us. We no longer have individual Sunday School classes or interactive Bible study, so the people don't get a chance to ask questions. The confessional allows for deeper questions about God, and it's where they can get quality counsel. I agree with the bishop; it's not for money-making."

Removing my wallet from my pants pocket, I rifle through it, pulling out receipts and staring at them intently. The bishop takes the hint that I'm dismissing Pastor Dowling, so he ends the meeting while instructing me to be more considerate of my fellow man. How much more considerate could I be? Geraldine and I sold the home where we raised our three children last year. Although we should've gotten a one-bedroom apartment, we got two bedrooms to have one room for the grandkids. We sold her car and are down to one car. My poor Geraldine has been forced to buy makeup from a dollar store since she can no longer afford her name-brand cosmetics. This life we're living is below what children of God should settle for.

Despite wanting to go home, it's my turn to sit in the confession booth. It baffles me that the bishop is against face-to-face counseling, claiming anonymity makes people more forthcoming. I know who the voices belong to, but perhaps the members convince themselves I don't. I'm a man of God and would never tell the members' secrets. The bishop should have more faith in his staff.

Once inside the confessional, a lady enters wearing too much perfume. It's Mrs. Tanner. This is what I mean. There's always a way of identifying the person.

She says, "It's tax season again. Last year, we talked about my reasons for stealing. I've learned a lot from you, but I fear I'll lie again on my taxes. It's tempting to claim kids who aren't mine. Tax season is the only time I live like a queen, buying my heart's desires. Am I going to hell?"

If I told her she was going to hell, would it make her stop? I'll never know because I'm a professional. I've never had counseling training, but the word of God and common sense hasn't failed me yet.

"Only God knows if you're going to hell, but your behavior isn't pleasing to Him. You win now, but what happens if you get caught?"

"I'd be embarrassed," she says. "I've been trying to get my family to come to church, but if they found out what I'm doing, they'll call me a hypocrite and never visit here. I couldn't live with that."

Now, she's using her brain. Let me push further. "If they called you a hypocrite, would there be any truth in it?"

She takes a minute to consider. "I don't like to think about it, but yes. I have a cousin who shoplifts, and I'm always on her about stopping it. I tell her she should be happy with what she has."

"Is it possible that you should be happy with what you have?"

"You're right, Pastor. How do I stop? The woman whose kids I claim every year has already texted me."

"I won't lie. It's hard passing up easy money. However, ask yourself who do you want to be: God's representative or a hypocrite. Things like this have a way of getting revealed."

"I have to think about other ways of making an income so I can live well all year." She's now on to something. This is what I like about my job: the ability to make a difference.

"What are you passionate about these days? Or what did you like doing when you were a child?" I ask.

"I've never been good at anything. This is why I resort to lying on my taxes. I'm pathetic and have never had interests." If I don't turn this around, she'll be cheating the government again.

"Glory to God. I just had a vision of colorful quilts. Do quilts mean anything to you?" I lie about the vision because I'm not supposed to know who I'm talking to. She made a quilt for my wife a few years ago, and it's on our bed today. It's of good quality, and I've never known why she doesn't sell them. My wife said the quilt is worth a few hundred dollars.

"A vision." Mrs. Tanner chuckles. "I haven't made quilts in a while but selling them could increase my income. There are places online where I could sell them. My daughter could help, I guess."

She thanks me and exits the confessional. Another life sent in the right direction. Now it's up to her what she'll do next. After seeing several more churchgoers, I collect my things and go home.

MY HOME IS empty and lonely. Geraldine is working late; I must eat without her. Frustrated that I suck at being a provider, I go to the backyard and smoke a cigarette. I quit a long time ago but started again when Geraldine went back to work. I shouldn't get down on myself, but I can't stop feeling like a failure. If a church member were going through the same thing, I'd remind the individual to lean on God. It's not like I'm not relying on God to supply my needs. I trust Him. Yet, the cigarette takes the edge off and feels good between my fingers.

When I finish smoking, I warm up baked beans and hot dogs. It sounds gross, but the hot dogs come from grass-fed beef Geraldine found on sale. I'd like vegetables, but Geraldine seldom buys them these days because they go bad too quickly, and we can't afford to waste money.

THE NEXT DAY, I get to church early since it's my day to clean the pews and vacuum. Other churchgoers volunteered in the past and were faithful for a short time before flaking. All I do these days is complain. If I'm not telling Geraldine how I feel, I think about my grievances. The bishop should call out the lazy members, but he doesn't, at least not directly. On occasion, he'll add in his sermon how the Lord needs faithful servants in the church as if that's supposed to convict anyone. If it were up to me, I'd stand over the pulpit and give examples of all the problems and tell people to get off their asses and help. I regret saying ass. Sometimes, I get worked up over things that may never change. Well, I shouldn't assume things. The bishop is getting up in age. Perhaps he'll pass on the ministry to one of us younger brothers. Since the bishop is in his early seventies, I'd imagine he'd be talking with the staff about stepping down and naming his successor, but he hasn't. And I haven't worked up the nerve to bring it up. He can be sensitive, and I'm not his favorite person. I wouldn't want him to think I'm praying for his death. Yet, if he were out of the way, I could have more say. For me to have such thoughts, it could mean the Lord is planning on taking the bishop home so we can bring new ideas to the church. He doesn't understand the current generation, which is why the church suffers. Attendance isn't what it used to be, so the offering is down. The church members won't say why others have left the ministry, but I have my suspicions. The bishop makes the choir sing songs from back in his day, and if they sway too much, he swears they're behaving worldly. I'm in my fifties, far from young, but I'm not set in my ways like the bishop.

After cleaning, I eat my bologna sandwich and chips before stepping inside the confessional. Brother Henderson enters and brings me up to date. "Forgive me, Pastor, for I have sinned. I haven't told my wife about the strip club like you advised. It's the right thing to do, but I fear she'll leave me."

The thing I don't like about this job is that people hear what they want. I never told Brother Henderson to tell his wife. I simply asked how she might act if she finds out. If it were me, I wouldn't tell Geraldine. "Is that what you heard me say? I recall suggesting you stop the behavior because it's bringing you so many problems."

"Maybe I misheard, and guilt is plaguing me. My wife needs things around the house, but I don't buy them because I'm throwing money at the strip club. But there's a part of me that likes watching women twerk and bounce in my lap. My wife doesn't do those things. She plays gospel music the few times we do have sex."

My heart goes out to him. I wouldn't know how to react if Geraldine held back in bed. She enjoys sex as much as she did during our first few years together. If she ever plays gospel during lovemaking, I'd run out of the house. Strippers could teach the church sisters a thing or two. It's an un-Godly thing to say, but true. His wife is acting too holy, and now my dear brother is at the club, making butt cheeks wiggle. How do I approach this tactfully? "Have you talked to your wife about your sexual needs?" I'm not ashamed to ask tough questions. Some Christians downplay sex, but not me. Studies show that most marriages end because of finances and lack of sex. I'd be doing the married congregation a disservice if I didn't have these conversations.

"I've never had a formal sit-down, but I often ask for sex, and she's tired from working. I get it. She works, and so do I, but I have needs. I've not had sex with anyone at the strip club, but it's tempting. My wife wears bonnets and charcoal face masks to bed."

"If you want things to change at home, be direct with your wife. I'm not saying volunteer the information about the strippers; that's up to you. However, if she asks, tell the truth. Say you are sexually frustrated and want more sex and for her to initiate it sometimes. Tell her to throw out that bonnet and face cream. Take a gentler tone with her, though, but you know what I'm saying. You're playing a dangerous game with the strippers. I'm a man. I get the need for sex and visual stimulation; don't misunderstand me."

"So, you are saying if it were you, you'd tell her you're not satisfied?"

I answer truthfully, "I sure would. For men, sex is a need, not a want, as the late great Pastor Myles Munroe once said. If she doesn't give it to you, at least you know you tried. Some women drive their husbands into the arms of other women due to lack of sex. If you cheat without having this conversation with your wife and giving her a chance to fix the problem, you're at fault."

"You might be right." We talk about other stressors in his life, and when we're done, he passes me a twenty-dollar bill. I accept it, although the bishop doesn't want us taking money for our services. This twenty will buy Geraldine and me some fruit and vegetables. Before putting the money in my wallet, I stare at it, wondering how many butt cheeks it's been in at the strip club.

I'M in the bishop's office the following day because Brother Henderson told him he gave me money and needed it back but was too embarrassed to tell me. I'm assuming Brother Henderson gave me the funds he planned on giving the strippers. Now I'm in the office, embarrassed, and for what? I haven't done anything wrong.

"Don't let this happen again," the bishop says. "This is the reason I advise against accepting money. We don't want to put ourselves in compromising situations with our members. Let them show gratitude by placing money in the collection box versus in our hands. Do you understand?"

"You won't have this problem from me again." This is ridiculous. Even though Brother Henderson is foul, I'll treat him no differently when I see him. I won't even bring it up. I only wish he had come to me. Now I feel like a liar and a thief, and the only thing I did was accept a love offering. I hope the bishop talked to Brother Henderson about not being stingy. Everything in me wants to expose why Brother Henderson might need the money, but I take confidentiality seriously. Plus, the bishop would reprimand me.

I pray silently for Brother Henderson. "Dear God, let a big booty stripper fart in Brother Henderson's face while his face is between her cheeks. Amen."

The bishop extends his hand for the money, but I don't have it. Yesterday, I went to the grocery store after church. How embarrassing for a man not to have twenty dollars in his wallet. "Don't worry. I'll take it out of your next check." The bishop stands, indicating it's time for me to go.

It may be petty, but I go into the sanctuary and text Geraldine about what happened. Of course, I refrain from saying the church member's name. I can always count on Geraldine, who assured me I did right. Unlike me, she thinks the bishop likes me.

Despite not feeling up to counseling anyone, I go to the confessional booth. It's my calling; if I stop, I'll disappoint God. The bishop and my late father ingrained in me to finish what I started, making me faithful to a fault. Many people at this church don't have my work ethic, and it shows. Luckily, I have a dutiful wife. Without her love and devotion, I'd give up hope for humanity.

A few minutes later, Brother Nick enters the booth, a young man new to the church who always speaks to me after service. He doesn't serve in any ministries, and I want to keep it that way. We need help here, but not that bad.

"The devil is controlling me every day," says Brother Nick. "You suggested I resist my urges, but they're strong. Every day, my neighbor gets in and out of her car, and her body calls to me. That's why it's difficult not to peek into her windows at night."

"What's going to happen once you get caught? I don't think you ask yourself that enough."

He says smugly, "I won't get caught. I've been doing it since she moved in. She's single and lives alone; no one will suspect me. I help with her groceries and always wave to her. She often says I'm a good young man." He laughs like he gets a kick out of deceiving others.

The young man is weird, and I'm happy my daughters aren't his age, or I'd strangle the prick. "Pride comes before the fall. If you like her so much, why not ask her out?" A normal person would do right by the neighbor, but he's far from normal. My question is useless now that I think of it.

"That would take the fun away from it. Like I said, it's the devil using me. The evil being in me enjoys that my neighbor believes I'm good. I'm tricking her, and I feel powerful. Only you and I know what lies beneath my façade. It might not be easy for you to understand, but it's a thrill for me. I don't have to ask her permission to watch her get naked through her sheer curtains. I watch her and imagine I'm there touching, stroking, licking—"

I interrupt. I'm normally non-judgmental. "I get it. You get a kick out of it. Do you want help?"

"Sure. Why else would I come to you? However, I like what I'm doing and don't know if I can quit. Only God can help me. I believe God and the devil will have to arm wrestle for my soul, and whoever wins will determine the man I'll be."

"If you're serious about help, see a psychiatrist or therapist with more experience than me. I'm happy you trust me, but this is outside of my scope. I'll pray for you, but those urges might need medication, which I don't have." Normally, I'm convinced God can handle any problem that comes to this booth, but Brother Nick might need psychiatric help to fight his urges.

"Are you trying to get rid of me?"

Clearly, he's not listening. "I want to ensure the safety of you and your neighbor. Have you done anything violent in the past?" Let's see if he tells the truth.

"I have a juvenile record, but it's behind me, and I won't talk about it."

Just what I thought. The peeping tom has a record. Wouldn't surprise me if he's attacked and raped women. He seems like the type. "You can keep coming to talk to me, but try harder to avoid that woman. Let's pray." After leading him in prayer and attempting to cast out the demons, I give up. Whatever evil entity living within him keeps laughing when I tell it to come out in the name of Jesus. Feeling like a failure, I advise him to keep the faith and go in peace.

LATER, I'm on the couch, and Geraldine is behind me, giving me a shoulder massage. "Why are you so tense?" she asks, kissing my neck.

I fill her in on the day.

"Honey, I wish you could call the police on that boy. I'd feel terrible if he killed or violated someone and we knew and said nothing."

"Geraldine, you're guessing his identity. We must trust God." I sound like the bishop, talking about trusting God.

"You don't have to tell me who it is. It's that new, weird young man. Creepiness oozes from his pores, making my skin crawl. He's good-looking, but something sinister is underneath. It's something women can feel. His neighbor has turned off her womanly power of spotting pervs; she'd better turn it back on before it's too late. I couldn't imagine him helping me carry groceries inside the house. Yuck."

Geraldine is big on trusting her women's intuition. She taught our daughters to rely on that inner warning, and they've been doing good so far. They both married good men who take care of home and provide well. Men like me, I might add. I'd like to think I had something to do with how our girls turned out.

Hours later, Geraldine and I make love, and she teaches me a new position. At my age, I surprise myself that I can do it. When I ask where she learned it, she says she and her best friend were talking about sex, and her friend told her about it. I can't be mad at all. What a delight to have my wife, who is also in her fifties, willing and ready to spice things up in the bedroom. I thank God I'm not Brother Henderson, in the strip club, motorboating women.

IT'S SUNDAY MORNING, and it's almost time for church dismissal. I sit in my usual seat behind the bishop, expecting him to thank everyone for coming like he does every week. But today, he does something different. "It's with great regret that I inform you that the church doors will be closing at the end of next month," says the bishop.

Did he say what I think he said? The confused look on everyone's faces and the grumblings confirmed I heard him right. How could he do this to me? There should have been a meeting to discuss this. I shouldn't be hearing this for the first time with the congregation. I turn to Pastor Dowling, and from the looks of it, this isn't news to him, which further convinces me that the bishop has it in for me. I step to the bishop at the pulpit, not caring who hears. "You think it's all right to surprise me like this? Where is the loyalty? How long have you known about this? Don't lie."

"I understand you're angry and surprised. There was no easy way to do it, so I'm letting everyone know at the same time."

"You're a damn lie!" I shout, and the people gasp as if they don't curse outside of the church. I point to Pastor Dowling. "He knew in advance. You can't convince me otherwise."

"Don't question me in front of the people, boy. Show respect," says the bishop like he's talking to a child, rather than to someone he's been disregarding for years.

This was the first time he referred to me as a boy. I wouldn't have accepted it any other day, and surely not today since it's my last day on the job. I don't care if we have a few more weeks before we close, I'm done. I snatch the microphone from him and exit the pulpit. Addressing the congregation, I say, "You lazy, cheap fools are why we're in this position. All you all do is take. Would it have killed you to pay tithes regularly or to give offerings? I watch your giving, and all I see is a bunch of dollars placed in the offering. You all are pathetic." I stop talking when Pastor Dowling snatches the microphone from my hand.

"You're out of line, Pastor Tom. Stop this foolishness." Pastor Dowling returns to the pulpit, assuming he put an end to me voicing my frustrations.

Before I can give chase to take back the microphone, Geraldine comes to my side, trying to console me. "Let's go home. Everyone is looking at us, and I don't want to be embarrassed further."

I scan the church, and all eyes are on me. This has nothing to do with my wife. I might never see these people again; I have things to get off my chest. To hell with confidentiality. These people would let me and my wife get evicted and starve; why should I care about them? Geraldine and I have given up so much, and I refuse to accept a handout from our kids. I point at Mrs. Tanner, whose mouth drops in shock. I don't need the microphone to project my voice. "You're lying to the government about your taxes, but I see your church giving around tax time hasn't increased. Why is that? You're claiming three or four kids that aren't yours. You can't give more to the Lord? How long will you keep stealing from God?" Mrs. Tanner runs out of the church. She impresses me; I didn't think she could move fast.

The bishop shouts at me from the pulpit, and Geraldine and Pastor Dowling pull at my arm. When I tear away from them, they back up. Nosey church members stare at me in anticipation, waiting for what I'll say next. Some who've told me juicy details in the past stand to leave, rightly suspecting they might be next. "Deacon Troy, slow down." I laugh at the way he's pulling his wife behind him. "Are you afraid I'll tell everyone that last year you discovered that your twenty-year-old daughter Keisha was having sex with your married thirty-something-year-old neighbor? Keisha wouldn't stop when you confronted her, and you kept letting her sing in the choir. Okay, leave then." I wave to their backs when they exit. I say to the congregation, "Deacon Troy is another one who signs up to clean the church but never shows up."

A few people, including Geraldine, advise me to put an end to whatever it is I'm doing. I don't listen. I have nothing to lose. Sister Liz is in the pew, shaking her head at me, so I walk to the end of her pew and say, "I don't care how many cakes you bake for Deacon Longfellow, he'll never marry you." Appalled, she grabs her necklace. I point at the deacon who stands on his row, daring me to keep talking. I don't scare easily, so the daggers he shoots at me don't stop me. "Someone cut his penis off years ago before he came to the Lord. Man caught him in bed with his wife. The deacon wasn't a deacon at the time, so don't hold the cheating against him. But, Sister Liz, he can't give you no deep loving, if you know what I mean. That's why he remains single." Several men hold back Deacon Longfellow. I would've kept the secret, but he's another one who is unfaithful to the ministry, and I caught him talking about me behind my back to the bishop before. The deacon doesn't like me, and I feel the same about him. I shake my head when some brothers escort Deacon Longfellow out of the church.

Look who's headed to the door. "Brother Henderson, may I have a word? Are you rushing off to put some more money in Big Booty Judy's booty?" Brother Henderson denies knowing what I'm talking about. "Don't lie, brother. God don't like ugly." I turn to his saintly wife. "He's not at home as much because he's spending money on strippers. He says you're frigid since coming to Jesus, and he must get stimulated elsewhere. Throw out the bonnets if he hasn't told you." When she cries, I shrug. Hopefully, the tears represent a knowing that she should do better. A few brothers are holding Brother Henderson back. If he knows like I know, he had better not put his hands on me. Fighting in church is unholy, but I'll make an exception today.

Geraldine is screaming at me, and so are some of the others. To get away from my wife, I walk to the other side of the church. I have more to say and saved the best for last. "Brother Nick, you should've left. Mr. McCreepy. Did you think I'd spare you?"

He yells, "Shut your mouth, old man! This ain't what you want."

Does he think I fear him? I call it how I see it. Geraldine is crying, and her friend is consoling her like I'm the bad guy. "Geraldine, stop crying. Our silence has gotten us nothing but into the poor house. You'll thank me later."

"Stop this foolishness, Tom. This is the Lord's house!" shouts Geraldine.

Ignoring her, I return my attention to Brother Nick, who stands to leave. "Don't go peeking into any other neighbors' windows after service. Stop jacking off to the sweet women on your block." He looks like he wants to kill me, but I stare at him back, wishing he'd try something. Before coming to Jesus, I was good with these hands. I'm not a woman, so I don't have to worry about him touching me.

Tossing my keys at Geraldine, I say, "Drive yourself home. I need time alone." I exit the church with people whispering and some shouting obscenities at me. I don't care what anyone thinks. I freed those people today. Their sins are out in the open, and now they can be better Christians if they choose. I can't believe the bishop has driven me to expose the church. Had he not taken me off guard, I might not have responded the way I did.

Outside, Brother Nick gives me the finger from his car. I don't bother responding. Brother Henderson and his wife are in their car arguing. I don't feel guilty at all. If they do the work needed, their marriage will be stronger.

To destress, I walk aimlessly until I land at a park, where I spend hours figuring out my next move. I'll find a new church, but in the meantime, I'll get a real job that pays well and has benefits. After more reflection, I still didn't feel bad about exposing the church. Because of them, I am jobless. And if Geraldine doesn't forgive me, I'm headed to divorce court.

Soon after, I make it home and don't have my house keys. I forgot to remove them when I gave Geraldine my car keys. To my surprise, the door is cracked. We never leave our door open. Stepping inside, I find my loving wife on the floor, stiff, lying in blood, with her panties and bra on the side of her and her dress pulled over her head. Blood trickles from her stomach. It looks like she has been stabbed repeatedly in the stomach. Screaming, I run to her, "Geraldine! Get up, baby." She doesn't answer. She can't be dead. I couldn't live without her, and our children and grandchildren would be devastated.

Dropping to my knees, I shake her. When she doesn't move, I remove her dress from her face, assuming she's in too much pain to do it herself. The shock in her dead eyes is too much to bear. Why? Who'd do this to her? She's loved by everyone, and she wouldn't harm a soul. My eyes travel to her stomach. There's something carved in her stomach: Devil did it.

That bastard!

I must take her to a hospital. Maybe they can resuscitate her. When I lift her, there's a lot of blood underneath her. She's been stabbed multiple times in the back. Defeated, I lay her down and hold her hand, praying that the Lord will take me too. Why would Nick come after her and not me? This isn't fair.

Someone is clapping. Brother Nick comes from the kitchen with a sharp knife in his hand. "You like my work, old man? Sister Geraldine sure felt good when I was inside of her. I've never been with an old woman, but now they're all I want." He licks his fingers as if he's remembering his time with Geraldine.

"I'll kill you!" Before I can get to my feet, Nick knocks me down and lands the knife in my chest. When I stumble, he stabs me multiple times, sending the most intense pain I've ever felt throughout my body.

He turns me on my back. "What did we learn?" I can't talk, but I'd curse him out if I could. He places a finger over his lips as if he knows I have words for him. "Shhh. I'll answer for you. We learned that whatever is said in the damn booth stays in the damn booth." Raising his hand, he plunges the knife into my chest. The last thing I see is the evil thing that lives inside Nick.

The End

acknowledgments

Thank you, God, for the gift of storytelling. Shout out to Ebony Evans from EyeCU Reading & Chatting Facebook Group. Ebony invited me to participate in Freestyle Friday, where selected authors showcase short story writing skills. Authors receive the story title on a Friday morning and must write and post the story the same day. "Family Meeting" was my title, which I've included in this collection. I've used other Freestyle Friday titles in this collection: New Year, New Me… Now What?, Exposed, and If You're Reading This Letter. If you're searching for a group to connect with other readers, EyeCU Reading & Chatting is a fantastic book club made up of authors and readers who share a love for all things literary. Check them out: EyeCU Reading & Chatting | Facebook

These stories are an homage to a few of my favorite shows: *Alfred Hitchcock Presents*, *The Alfred Hitchcock Hour*, *The Twilight Zone*, *Tales from the Crypt*, *Tales from the Darkside*, *The Hitchhiker*, and *Are You Afraid of the Dark?*

Thank you, beta-readers, for your invaluable input on my stories: Maddy D., Kelly Kirkland, Talese Nicole, Sam O, and Amy Shakeel Randolph-Beach. Thank you to my readers. I truly appreciate your support which motivates me to keep writing. I hope to continue entertaining you for many years to come.

afterword

Did you enjoy *Twisted Endings*?

If so, please consider leaving an online review. To get updates about new releases, follow me on Amazon: https://www.amazon.com/author/samyraalexander . You can also follow me on BookBub: Samyra Alexander Books - BookBub .

Website:
www.samyraalexander.com
Facebook:
Samyra Alexander Author Page | Los Angeles CA | Facebook
Instagram:
Samyra Alexander (@tellsamyra) • Instagram photos and videos
Email:
tellsamyra123@gmail.com

also by samyra alexander

I Should Have Worn a Curtain: A psychological fiction novella

I Should Have Worn a Curtain 2: A psychological fiction novella

Road To Malevolence

Road To Malevolence 2

The Predator's Prey

Hardened Hearts: A psychological drama

about the author

Samyra Alexander, author of the popular and addictive series, *I Should Have Worn a Curtain*, has always flourished in the art of verbal storytelling. Samyra's love of reading lit a creative spark, inspiring her to pen books in the genres of psychological and contemporary fiction.

Samyra was born and raised in Gary, Indiana, and lives in Los Angeles. She holds a doctorate in Clinical Psychology and enjoys exploring mental health issues and their accompanying taboos within the context of creative fiction. When she's not working as a psychotherapist, Samyra dedicates herself to creating memorable characters readers want to strangle.

www.ingramcontent.com/pod-product-compliance
Lightning Source LLC
Chambersburg PA
CBHW051856130726
47987CB00002B/863